THE SPAHIS

A boat sails into an African port, carrying a curious cargo of beggars. These men, underdogs in the States of Arabia, are ready to rebel and carve out their own kingdom. Striking whilst the ruling sheik is at war with the French, they join a group of American deserters from the Foreign Legion of France. However, when Mahmoud and his Bedouins retake land, too confidently taken from them, it seems that the game is up for these desperate allies.

GORDON LANDSBOROUGH

THE SPAHIS

Complete and Unabridged

LINFORD
Leicester

First published in Great Britain

First Linford Edition
published 2013

British Library CIP Data

Landsborough, Gordon.
 The Spahis. - - (Linford mystery library)
 1. War stories.
 2. Large type books.
 I. Title II. Series
 823.9′14–dc23

 ISBN 978–1–4448–1438–5

Published by
F. A. Thorpe (Publishing)
Anstey, Leicestershire

Set by Words & Graphics Ltd.
Anstey, Leicestershire
Printed and bound in Great Britain by
T. J. International Ltd., Padstow, Cornwall

This book is printed on acid-free paper

1

'Your Turn, *Mon Ami!*'

The little white town seemed to cling around the blue Mediterranean bay as if in fear of that mighty, encroaching desert to the west of it. It lay there in the brilliant sunshine of that summer afternoon, and scarcely a breath of wind came to stir the standard that drooped limply from the flagstaff over the sugar-cake palace on the mound to the north of the town.

It had been built there long ago by a despot who feared the smells of the town as much as some of its oppressed inhabitants. And it was more of a fortress than a palace, and even now, in the absence of its tyrannical ruler, there were sentries posted at every ornate gateway.

There was one there now, a true son of the desert in his flowing white burnouse, lean of face and with the black, pointed

1

beard that is fashionable among the Bedouin.

He stood insolently in the shadow from a high gatepost, and his contemptuous eyes looked down over the town and upon the few inhabitants who were out at that unfavourable hour.

They were mostly beggars and homeless peasants and people who had to work, even though to do so in that torrid sunshine was sickening. And because they were of this menial class, that soldier-sentry could accordingly look down upon them.

If he had been more alert he might have wondered that, this day, there appeared to be more astir in the squalid little town than was usual. But his thoughts weren't on the scene before him.

He was thinking of his comrades, who had ridden with their leader, the great Sheik Mahmoud ibn Kalim ibn Achmet ibn Hussein el Dusa. They had answered a call to war to drive out the French who occupied the northern Arab territory.

There had been exciting days in this little province of Hejib, this tiny Arab state on the shores of the blue Mediterranean. Sheik Mahmoud had called to arms the Faithful, and he had ridden round the town calling the people his brothers and urging them forward to receive arms so that they could go and fight for their country.

He had told them that death in this cause was gallant, and they would find their reward in heaven. He had been persuasive, even though normally he had all the tyrant's contempt for the common herd. He had hidden his real feelings, and then he had gone out with his army to join others in a desert campaign that would surely bring death to many of the townspeople.

But he hadn't taken all his loyal bodyguard. He could not trust his people, and so it was that many of his faithful followers had to remain behind to guard his palace to see that upstarts did not deprive Sheik Mahmoud of his possessions in his absence.

Thinking of these precautions, which had deprived him of the thrills and excitement of a desert campaign, the

Arab warrior shrugged. These curs wouldn't dare try to overthrow their master, he thought. And though they were few, this bodyguard that had been left behind, he felt sure they could stop any attempt at insurrection — this revolt that was continually upon the lips of the poorer classes who were taxed beyond endurance and were deprived of a justice which they were beginning to assert was rightfully theirs.

His brown eyes surveyed the harbour, where a rusty old tramp steamer was tied up at a wharf. It had been tied to that wharf for the last two days, an unlovely thing, without a scrap of paint on its rusting, rotting hulk.

The Arab sentry, musing idly to himself, realised that in all the time it had been down there, he had never once seen a sign of life from it. That was curious, because these tramp steamers usually discharged an assorted cargo and then very quickly got out of this little port of Dusa, in the Hejib.

It was at this moment in his thoughts that he heard a pattering of feet behind him, and when he turned he saw a comrade hastening at unusual speed considering the heat of that afternoon. And that lean, hawk-like desert warrior's face was suffused with excitement.

The sentry turned to greet him, because in this town there was little that could excite a man's mind. He hoped for interesting news — and he got it.

The newcomer stabbed his finger towards that rusty old tramp steamer, and he said: 'Know you, O brother, that that ship lies there because of an act of piracy on the high seas?'

It startled the sentry. His eyes flickered towards that ship, and it was just at that moment that for the first time he saw life aboard.

A fluttering white robe could be seen moving across the deck. Then it began to cross a small, precarious gangway that gave access to the littered quayside.

'News has just reached us over the radio,' said the newcomer, and he was prolonging this moment, enjoying the importance that comes when there is an interesting tale to tell and an impatient listener wanting to know it.

His head jerked towards a tower where an aerial was slung. Sheik Mahmoud was up to date in many ways, and he had both transmitter and receiver in that radio tower.

'And that news, O man of slow tongue?' the sentry asked sharply.

'It seems that a boat has put in to Dema,' his informant continued, unperturbed by the impatience of his companion. 'In it was the master and his officers of this ship which now lies in Dusa harbour. They told a tale of how, when they were two days out from Alexandria, there was a sudden revolt on the part of the passengers whom he was carrying along this coast.

'It seems that he had been transporting over a hundred poor, ill-clad sweepings of the gutter. They were paying him to transport them to Sollum, though they gave no reason for wanting to go so far from the gutters of their native Alexandria.

'But when they were near Sollum, as I have said, all in one moment those

6

passengers rose as one man and forced the captain and his officers to take to a boat, where they were set adrift in the sea.'

'And what of the crew?' asked the sentry, his eyes resting broodingly on that rusting hulk.

He had noticed a further movement aboard the ship. Now several Arabs were flitting across the deck and coming ashore.

The crew? It seems they were at one with the pirates — for that was what they were, taking that ship away from its owner and master. The crew made no attempt to help their officers but, instead, it seems they were abusive and truculent to the men whom they had 'served'.

'It is the way of these scum,' said the sentry impatiently.

'It is the way of scum always,' agreed that second Arab. 'They fawn and wheedle and smile, but the moment they have the power to do so they become like poisonous reptiles towards their lords and masters. I do not understand it.'

They were not understanding men, in

any event. To them there were two kinds of people — the ones who gave orders, such as themselves, and the ones who obeyed.

Again they saw men coming ashore from that little ship, sweltering in the harbour. It seemed as though all who were aboard must for some reason at this moment be deciding to come ashore, and it aroused speculation in the minds of those two Arabs standing at the gateway to Sheik Mahmoud's palace.

The sentry posed the obvious question: 'O brother, what does our leader think about it?' For Sheik Mahmoud had left his cousin in charge of the palace in his absence, and it was this cousin who would give orders in regard to this unusual affair.

The second Arab shrugged.

'The news has reached us only this minute,' he said. 'And ibn Kalim sleeps, and it is not wise to waken a sleeper such as ibn Kalim.'

The sentry nodded understandingly. Ibn Kalim wakened always in a raging temper, and regardless who it was, anyone near at hand received the wrath of his tongue — and sometimes more. There was a man even now in the dungeons of this sprawling white palace who had done nothing more than stumble and make a noise outside Ibn Kalim's chamber, and thus awakened him.

He had been for ten days with nothing to eat and only enough water to keep him barely alive.

That was the kind of man ibn Kalim was . . . and yet he was an angel of mercy compared with the thin-faced, ambitious sheik, his cousin, who was now fighting across the Libyan border.

The two stood together for a while and discussed the matter, and made conjecture on ibn Kalim's actions when he discovered that a pirated ship was sitting right there in Dusa harbour. Both were agreed that this would be a glorious opportunity for ibn Kalim to use his whip and to torture and to throw into the deepest, dankest dungeons the perpetrators of this outrage.

They saw more Arabs coming ashore in their long fluttering robes. By now at least fifty must have crossed onto the quayside, and were disappearing into the alleys of this town just beginning to stir from its afternoon siesta.

The first man ashore had come through the smelly alleys towards the road which climbed between flat-topped mud buildings towards the magnificent gates of the palace.

He was a tall, straight Arab in the long simple gown of the fellahin, and it was worn and ragged and much soiled. He was a man of low parts obviously.

And yet he strode purposefully along, and his broad shoulders were squared and his head was held erect like a man who is proud and has no fear of anyone. His feet were bare, like those of any other common Arab worker.

He came to where a man sprawled in the shadow of a mud wall. The man was a beggar, and there was little life in him because he had eaten too little for too long. The big newcomer from the rusty ship in the harbour paused as he looked down upon the dozing, scrub-bearded beggar.

And then his bare foot reached out and his prehensile toes clasped about the foot of that sprawling beggar.

Like fingers they seized upon that leathery big toe and shook it gently.

The sleeper came uncomfortably out of his doze. Eyes flickered open. They were eyes that were dead, with hopes that had been killed many years before. They looked at that tall, rather brooding figure in the costume of the fellahin, and there wasn't even a question in the dull vacant orbs.

And then that Arab who stood over him pushed back the hood of his cloak, so that his face could be seen by the man on the ground — but by no others.

The beggar saw a fine face. He saw the face of a young man, a man who was as handsome as a god. It was a face in the classical Greek tradition: straight nose, broad between the eyes — and those eyes were blue, too — and there was intelligence on that noble countenance. He was Arab, for all that, and merely reflected the strain of Greek conquerors of several thousand years before.

But the beggar's eyes did not look for these racial strains, and weren't touched by the sight of such beauty on a man's face. Instead they focused slowly upon the forehead of that hooded man.

And then those eyes of the beggar widened, and for the first time in years there was the semblance of life in those listless eyes. Suddenly they snapped into alertness, and they were excited, and there was an eagerness in them that hadn't been there for years before. He even started to struggle into a sitting position, but a quick warning gesture from the tall Greek-like Arab stayed him where he was.

Then that Arab pulled back his hood and began to walk up the alley again, leaving a man with his mind in turmoil, but in fierce, warm happiness.

For a sign had come to that Arab beggar. He had seen something that day that had been whispered about in the bazaars and wherever poor men gathered. For long it had been promised, and now he had seen it with his own eyes . . . he had lived to the day so long promised the oppressed on this great continent.

He had seen a black diagonal cross, marked on the forehead of that tall stranger. The black cross that had been spoken of so often . . .

With shaking fingers that beggar crouched against the wall, fumbled into his rags and pulled out a small piece of charcoal that had been there these many months. He had thought he would never use it, but now was the time — now was the day!

He carefully marked himself like that big Greek-like Arab, with a diagonal black cross on his forehead.

He was just finishing this operation when Yusef the porter limped out from the house opposite — if such a hovel could thus be described.

Yusef limped because he had earned the displeasure of some minor official up at the palace, and he had been bastinadoed. The beating upon his feet had been more to provide a diversion to the bored and listless occupants of the palace than for a merited punishment. Either way, it had hurt Yusef, and he was still limping, because of the bruised under-soles of those tormented feet.

That pain-ridden man suddenly halted and it seemed that his body jerked stiffly erect, as if for a second the pain in his feet was completely forgotten. His eyes were fixed incredulously upon that black diagonal cross on the forehead of the beggar across the alley from him.

Yusef stumbled forward. His voice was so suppressed with excitement that it came as a croak from his lips — 'Today?' he asked.

The beggar's eyes were shining, almost grinning with the delight that was in his poor tormented soul. He could hardly find voice to whisper back the answer — 'Today! Allah be praised!'

At that Yusef looked round, and then fiercely his hand shot out and the beggar knew what the porter wanted. He leaned forward and put into that brown, toil-calloused hand that small piece of charcoal.

Yusef stood erect again, like a man who has suddenly found his freedom. With care he marked upon his forehead that black diagonal cross.

And then Yusef, almost without limping now because he was sustained by the excitement of this glorious day, went walking into the *fellahin* quarters back of this alley. The beggar watched him go and then, when he was out of sight, he lay there against the shadowy wall and he listened and he was content.

He heard suppressed exclamations, and then there began a stir in those low quarters, among the flat-topped mud-walled buildings. In time the sound became not unlike that of a disturbed and angry beehive — only there was no anger in this rising murmur of sound, only excitement.

Up at the palace-gates that sentry, alone now, with the curved sword on his shoulder as a gesture to the duty he had to perform, heard this murmuring, swelling sound and his perplexed brown eyes looked out over the area from which it came. It seemed to him that the noise was spreading and taking in other quarters until the whole of the lower part of the town around the harbour was filled with this buzzing noise.

It was not understandable, but there was no way just then of satisfying his curiosity.

He looked down the long hill, which led almost directly into the harbour area. There was a lone peasant trudging wearily in the sunshine towards him, and far behind him came others grouped together.

Suddenly his mind alerted, connecting those groups with the numbers that he had seen leaving that rusting ship in the harbour. He thought that these would be the same people.

He stirred at that, a feeling of unrest and excitement in his blood. Yet for the moment he did nothing to alert the rest of the guards inside that high palace wall. For the moment, anyway, there seemed no need for a warning cry, even though it was unusual to see such a large body of men climbing a steep hillside towards the palace in that hot hour of the afternoon. Again, he did not know for sure that these were the men reputed to have taken a ship from its lawful owners whilst out on the sea lanes. A man might make a fool of himself so easily, that proud young Arab sentry was thinking.

But he was alert and suspicious, and when that lone, trudging peasant came near, he called imperiously for the man to come across to him.

'O dog, what happens in the town that there should be this noise when wise men are still in their beds?' he demanded peremptorily.

He was watching those larger groups of peasants, but they were all far behind, far down the hillside at that moment. They did not represent any danger.

The big, hooded peasant came across at the sentry's call. He did not speak.

'Dog, hast thou no tongue?' the sentry asked irritably, his eyes on those groups ascending the hill.

Suddenly his eyes jerked towards this big, rather grim-looking figure. The peasant was still advancing towards him without speaking.

The sentry called abruptly: 'Stay where thou art, O gutter rat!'

The peasant marched on. The sentry's

eyes quickened with sudden suspicion and apprehension. He was noticing how big and erect and somehow commanding that lone figure was — there was something in his carriage that set him apart from other men broken and bent with the toil of their lives.

He shouted again: 'Halt!'

At that the peasant merely flung back the hood that covered his head, but he came walking on, and now the sentry saw that black diagonal cross marked on the high intelligent forehead.

That curved sword came leaping down, and it was whistling through the air in a threatening gesture to keep the advancing peasant at his distance.

Yet in some way, somehow, that big, erect man with the black cross on his forehead leapt inside that swinging sword arm — a hand came behind the sentry's burnoused neck and another hand pushed on the man's chin . . . and one of the bodyguard of Sheik Mahmoud, who was of the house of Husseini, was gathered to his fathers in an instant.

Not a sound had been made to betray

this interlude to the guard who lounged in the gardens beyond. The big peasant with the face like a Greek god caught that falling, suddenly limp body, and allowed it to slide to the ground. He stooped and picked up the sharp scimitar and then straightened and looked back at those advancing men on the hill. And then, quite calmly and patiently, he stood over the dead body and waited for his companions to approach him. As they came near — as ragged a crew of men as were ever to be found — he could see that all had the black cross marked upon their foreheads.

Down in the town that murmur had changed to an uproar, and now men were pouring out into this long, straight cobbled road which led up to the palace. The man who seemed obviously the leader of this revolt caught the flash of sunlight upon weapons and knew that the *fellahin* of the town had armed themselves.

But though they were his brothers they were rabble. It was these men who had come from the ship who were the trained fighters, the spearhead of this insurrection that was to shake the Arab continent.

They came towards him and they had the eyes of men about to risk all upon the most desperate of ventures.

It was obvious that they knew what to do, for without any signal they began to break up into little parties, as if each had a duty to perform.

The Greek who was no Greek now put on the robe of that sentry, and began to march four of the ragged crew through the wide gateway towards the tree-shaded front to one of the palace entrances. It was here that the palace guard was mounted, and here that the guard commander and his men off duty were at rest.

The Arab guard commander saw the little group approaching, and he grew angry, because it was not right that a sentry should leave his place to march in scum such as these. They should have been kept outside the gates, so that their grievances or whatever they were could be attended to later when the sun was cooler and he, the guard commander, felt disposed to walk out and speak to them.

Angrily he rose to his feet off the plaited mattress that was made of fine fibres from palm leaves. His men looked at him, but continued to recline because there was no apparent reason for them to rise.

The disguised sentry boldly marched his quartet of ragged men straight to the door of that guardroom. In a rage, the guard commander jumped to the door, shouting that he wanted no lice-ridden scum in his domain.

He never reached the door, and he never protested against lice any more — or their owners.

Five men sprang into the guardroom. The Greek caught the surprised guard commander by the loose wrapping of the burnouse around the throat, and he twisted expertly and it tightened, and the guard commander began to choke. After a while he went down on his knees, and then his head drooped, and then his body went limp and there was no more guard commander on earth.

The four ragged men seized the dozing

off-duty guards — there was a flash of steel, and in a moment the deed was done.

The intruders gathered together and looked at their leader. He was calm and unhurried, and there was not an ounce of fear in him. He was a man superbly confident in himself, and because of this he could command and men would obey.

Now he went to the doorway, and he lifted his hands, and at that those several other little parties ran into the palace courtyard, and each went and took up a position at some strategic place — by an open doorway, or by some shuttered window which could be opened and entered. Others went round to where guards were posted at the other entrances to the palace, and because they came unexpectedly from the rear, and in any event came with great stealth, they were not heard, and sentries were disposed of in a manner that was miraculously simple and effective.

It was at the moment when the last of the sentries was disposed of, when that entire wall was defenceless — and within the palace those who remained of Sheik Mahmoud's entourage slept on and were heedless and unaware — it was at this moment that a ragged fellow was seen to climb hand over hand up a rope which went to the flagstaff on the tower. And when he was aloft he pulled on a secondary rope and the flag of the house of el Dusa came down. There was a second's pause while that ragged man fumbled, and then another flag rose to the masthead.

It was a blood-red cloth, and over it was a black diagonal cross.

They must have been watching from that old ship stinking in the scummy waters of the harbour, for at once a puff of steam was seen to rise from its siren, and then distantly the prolonged blast came floating up the hillside, disturbing those who had slept on.

It must have been a signal, for the ascending mob on the hillside came suddenly sweeping like an avalanche in through the many gates of the tyrant's palace.

They came as rabbles do, with much shouting, and waving of weapons and rolling of eyes. They looked a hideous, frightening crew, but for a few seconds there was no one there to see them.

And then came the first warning shouts from within the palace, as someone spied the throng from behind a shuttered window. At once men leapt from their cushioned couches, and orders were shouted, and there was the sound of arms being taken up and men rushing to guard the doors.

From the harem, that secluded wing of the palace with its latticed windows, women began to scream in terror: for it was notorious that mobs invariably made for the women's quarters and took revenge on a tyrant through the females of his household.

When the menfolk who remained to garrison this fortress palace came by many ways down to the great hall from which all corridors and rooms radiated in the palace, they found that band of leading spirits in this insurrection already there — those ragged brethren with the black crosses on their foreheads.

There was savage fighting on winding

marble staircases, and there was blood soaking into rich, native carpets. There was the sound of guns exploding with a crashing echo and re-echo in that lofty hallway, and then the smoke bit into the contestants' noses and clouded their vision.

It was no fight. It had been too well-planned. This Greek, who had come out of the desert to meet a ship as it came, according to plan, into that little harbour, had schemed well, and nothing had gone wrong.

There were too few to guard too great a place, and they went down before these resolute men with the crosses on their brown foreheads. In ten minutes there was no resistance. But there were plenty of crosses, for these men had much to repay, and at this moment they seized upon an opportunity to get back at the tyrants who had made them what they were.

All at once there was looting throughout the palace, as men who had suffered all those years in this little State of Hejib thought to claim their own. Each man grabbed what he could, but that Greek with his followers who had stolen a ship because they had not the passage money for such a long journey up the African coast, stood aside and took nothing — and wanted nothing.

The Greek spoke softly to one of his lieutenants. He said: 'Let them take what they will. They have as much right to it as the man who calls himself owner.' He thought for a second, and then added: 'And every man who takes from Sheik Mahmoud must for evermore be the tyrant's enemy!'

It was good policy to let the rabble help themselves.

And then the Greek mounted the curving, marble staircase and went along the corridors to see that nothing had been overlooked. He came eventually to doors that were guarded by eunuchs, in the way that was traditional in the feudal Arab palaces. They were big, soft creatures, and when those fierce, be-crossed strangers came to the doors they stood aside and helplessly watched while men walked into the harem.

There were womenfolk within, and when the doors opened and they saw that motley throng they fled screaming into their rooms off this main hallway wherein they spent most of their lives.

The Greek looked at them hiding their faces as if sight of man would cast spells upon them. He was a man who had long been emancipated from the primitive superstitions of his people, and he ignored those gestures.

He wanted none of these women, in any event, because they were pampered creatures — women who lived most of their lives in darkness so that their skins would be pale and thus please their outdoor masters the more. And they lived like sloths, with slave women to do their work for them, and with an abundance of sweetmeats, which gave them the desirable plumpness that found favour in the Arab males' sight.

To the Greek, a man who had travelled and seen women of other lands, they were unhealthy, sickening creatures. For himself he preferred another type of woman.

But he was here to get a woman

— though that was for a purpose connected with his plan.

His men had no such feelings and would have gone and helped themselves to these wives and concubines of a tyrant, but this had not been part of the plan — not yet, anyway.

The Greek sought with those fine eyes of his among the womenfolk cowering out of sight and yet peeping all the while in dread fascination at the intruders.

He called: 'I want Souriya, daughter of the despot, Sheik Mahmoud.'

For a second not a woman moved, and then a girl stepped out and faced him, and she was angry, but there was no fear in her eyes.

She was wearing a Western riding kit under a loose-flowing Arab cloak, as if she had dressed preparatory to a ride in the desert with the coming of evening coolness. She was a fine, handsome girl, vivid in the way of these Arab women. Her hair was a glossy, wavy, black frame to a face that was brown and unlike that of any other woman in this harem. Her eyes were big, and just now there was a light in them that spoke of savage temper.

She was a girl who was used to giving orders and to being obeyed, and never in her life before had she been addressed in such a manner by beggars from the gutter.

She shouted, peremptorily: 'Who are you? By Allah, my father will tear your tongues out and leave you for the carrion crows to eat while yet alive!'

The Greek bowed ironically. 'We must wait until your father returns and then submit ourselves to our punishment,' he said.

Then he strode forward, like a man who has no time for finesse, and he caught her in arms that were so strong that she was incapable of resistance.

He picked her up and carried her, her legs kicking ineffectually, out of the harem and down those winding stairs. And what his followers did when he left that room he did not care.

It was when he came down onto the ground floor, where a shrill-voiced mob was tearing down curtains and dragging up priceless carpets and laying their hands on anything that was gold and silver and of value, that from outside came a shouted greeting.

That distant siren and the fluttering, blood-red flag with its black diagonal cross upon it had attracted other watchers from the desert.

There were a dozen of them, and they walked on bare feet and were, if anything, more ragged than this rabble of the Dusa gutters. They led two horses between, and on one was a lovely Arab girl, a prisoner. And though she was lovely, clearly, unmistakably, she was of peasant stock.

On that other horse was another kind of prisoner — a man, and he wore the uniform of an officer of the French Foreign Legion, though upon his head was the flowing *kafir*, the traditional headdress of the desert nomad. Incongruously on his nose were perched rimless glasses, which gave him a harmless, clerkish appearance.

Yet this man was no harmless clerk. He was a man who had bathed in blood — a man who had killed more men than any man alive in Africa at that moment.

The little party rode boldly to where the rabble still streamed in through those gates that had been a barrier against them all their lives. They knew they were safe and among friends, though curious looks were cast at that blue-uniformed enemy of the Arab people . . .

★ ★ ★

A man crept furtively round to the rear of the palace, where the stables were. He found a gateway unguarded — a small gate set into the wall and used by servants going into the fields — and he thought it remarkable that no guard should be upon this particular gateway.

In fact, the circumstances were so suspicious he thought it was a trap, and for a long time he remained in hiding, not trusting to go through that gateway in case savage enemies lurked beyond.

And then the tumultuous noise from the palace immediately behind him grew too much for him, and he knew he would be discovered if he continued to hide there.

He glided quickly towards the gateway, and sidled carefully round the broad wall-end. He was even more surprised when he looked beyond.

Someone had been careless. There was a fine Arab stallion tied to a tree just beyond, and it seemed to be ready-provisioned for a desert journey, for food and goatskins of water were tied behind the saddle.

He looked round quickly, but there was no one in sight. He could hardly believe his luck, and thought that Allah must be watching over him. He went quickly out and hoisted his flowing robes and got his foot into the stirrup, and then he was in the saddle and his heels were digging into that horse's sides, and he was going like the wind westwards — westwards towards his cousin, Sheik Mahmoud.

As he thrashed that horse he gritted his teeth, and thought: 'By Allah, these dogs will have the skin flayed from their backs!' And again he was astonished at the ease with which he, alone of all that household, had managed to escape from the beggars . . .

★ ★ ★

When they brought news of ibn Kalim's departure to the Greek, he nodded in satisfaction.

This was how it had all been planned. Then he went across to where the Legion officer prisoner was sitting his horse.

He said: 'Now, *mon ami*, it is your turn.'

2

The Secret Place

It had a name in Arabic but only one in that party could pronounce it. To the others it was known as the valley-where-men-go-blind.

All that afternoon they had sat a mile distant in the desert looking away from that great mountain of glistening white that was blinding to their eyes in the brilliantly reflecting sun. They knew it for what it was — a deposit of salt that had grown mountainous in size against that great rocky range through which a hidden river ran.

That river was fresh enough to drink, though tainted a little with the salt, which continued to be deposited when the sun evaporated the running water. Yet the body needed salt as well as water in this heat, and so it was prized, and now this party moved forward to fill their water bottles.

They went with the lengthening of

shadows, when the sun's rays no longer bounced like arrowed missiles along that winding valley which gave access to the hidden water supply. On a previous occasion they had had to negotiate this valley with cloths over their eyes to keep out the reflecting sun, but this time it was more comfortable.

Even so they were glad when they came at length to the great, dark, yawning entrance to a cave that had been worn by erosion into this deposit of salt. Within was shade and a coolness they rarely experienced on this mighty Sahara desert. And within would be so much water that they could bathe in it and drink their fill and there would still be all the water they needed for their bottles when they resumed their journey.

In that party was one Arab. He was as ragged a man as could be found on any continent, a big man with a face of incredible ugliness, so that to be named Suleiman the Hideous was not without justification.

Yet in spite of the scars that pulled his face and gave him a repulsive leer, there was intelligence and patience and even humour in his big brown eyes. He seemed to be leading the party, like a man who has been these ways many times before.

There were four men in uniform with that Arab guide, and it was the uniform of the hated French Foreign Legion. Their blue tunics were torn and stained by their adventures of many weeks out on the desert, and their white fatigue trousers were no longer of the whiteness that was demanded in garrisons such as Sidi-bel-Illah.

One of the four was a big blond man who rode his horse like a man accustomed to horseflesh between his legs. He was lean and as brown as a native at the moment, with the fineness that comes when a man has passed through many ordeals in a desert that gives little time for respite and comfort. And there were little ridged muscles along his jaw, which gave his face an expression of determination that amounted to toughness.

Yet he had good, level grey eyes, and he was clearly a man of character and a man with considerable mental resources. In fact the problem posed was why a man of his obvious calibre should be in a legionnaire's uniform; for the Legion was notorious for the poverty of the manhood that fled into its ranks.

Riding to his right like a man who is his watchdog was a man not nearly so tall but of considerable weight. He had a face that might be described charitably as homely. It had been pounded flat, and then someone had got to work on his ears and pinned them close to his big, craggy skull. He had the appearance of a prize-fighter, only his face said that he hadn't always won the fights.

The third man was somehow more youthful-looking, with blue eyes and cheeks that were curiously red for a man who had lived years in the desert. He had a brightness about him, which spoke of a quick and alert mind, and even now after a day's riding across that oven-like desert, he sat his horse in the manner of a man filled with curiosity by his surroundings.

The fourth legionnaire was a man who looked amiably simple, a man slow of thought but good-natured in his outlook.

He had Nordic-blue eyes, like three of his comrades, and a face that was soft and going fleshy.

By the way he sat his saddle he seemed in some pain, and there was a black patch on his tunic, which could have been dried blood. Yet though he was still suffering from the effects of an Arab bullet wound, he never complained.

The fifth member of the party was a girl . . .

They rode up that winding valley between the salt hills with gladness on their faces, and yet they rode with their hands on their Lebel rifles, like men who are always afraid of treachery. The big legionnaire who came on the heels of Suleiman the Hideous was looking for tracks that would tell a story under the feet of their horses; but there was such a trampled confusion, as of the passing of many men and many horses, that at length he gave up the instinctive quest.

Instead his eyes became narrow and hard as they stared into that single black eye that was the cave entrance to the underground water supply. He was thinking to himself: 'Anything can happen in this desert!'

And then suddenly his scalp seemed to prickle as the hair rose on his skull. For he had realised something that his companions had missed.

A man should have shouted in Arabic for them to stay where they were — either that or send a shot over their heads.

But no man shouted. No man revealed himself in that cave entrance.

The big legionnaire pulled back on his horse and abruptly called to the Arabs who was leading them: 'Hold on, there!'

Suleiman turned his face towards the man who had spoken — a man who spoke with the nasal accent of an American. In that reddening light of evening there were long shadows on Suleiman's face where the scars were, making it more distorted and hideous than ever.

But the American legionnaire didn't see the mutilation of that face. By now he knew his guide well, and he knew that behind that tortured face was a man of one character. He was prepared to trust himself with Suleiman anywhere, though most people would have crossed the road to avoid a man of such forbidding aspect.

Suleiman called back in an English that held a curious accent; but then Suleiman, until he had tried to preach democracy and had been picked up and beaten by the political police of a dictator-country, had been a student in a Scottish university. He was a paradox, this beggar of beggars with the cultured accent of a university under-graduate.

'You spoke, Tex?' There was the faintest hint of impatience in his voice, for he wanted to be in at that water, for the day's thirst had hold of him now, and it was almost unendurable.

Tex was looking ahead. His lean brown hands were gripping his Lebel tightly. He said: 'Your fellars must have gone to sleep, Suleiman, or they'd be out an' at us by now, I reckon.'

Tex's grim, grey, slitted eyes darted quickly into the shadow of those salt hills on either side of the cavern, but he saw no movement and was reassured. His eyes came back to that black hole that was so much blacker because of the whiteness all around it.

His three legionnaire companions halted beside him, and the girl — blonde and blue-eyed and with the poise that comes to Western stock that believes in itself, asked: 'What's the matter, Tex? Are you scared of something?'

She said it in the manner of one who respected his hunches; for she knew that big Tex, the legionnaire from Texas, didn't scare easily and unnecessarily.

They all looked at that cave mouth as Tex said, in growling, uneasy tones : 'Suleiman's brothers should be here now. If they're here why haven't they come out to speak with us?'

For Suleiman was one of a brotherhood — the Brotherhood of Tormented Men — and this was one of their secret hideouts in the desert. Suleiman was bringing them to it because here was a man the legionnaires wanted.

Legionnaire Tex had joined the French Foreign Legion not to take up arms in a foreign cause, but to find a man reputed to be an officer in the Legion, a man wanted by the Allied War Crimes Commission.

He was a man known as Herman Sturmer, and he had killed in atrocious manner a thousand trapped American prisoners during the African campaign in the 1940s.

Suleiman had promised to bring them to the Brotherhood's hideout, because they had saved his life and befriended him in the desert. And Captain Herman Sturmer was a prisoner with the Brotherhood, and Suleiman had said that Sturmer would be handed over to the legionnaires, who could take him to the coast and then smuggle him to Britain or America for trial for his crimes.

So they had come across that great desert, with its Arab and French armies at war with each other, and they had risked their lives because now they were 'on pump' — that is, they were deserters — and they were expecting to be greeted by Suleiman's brethren.

So Legionnaire Tex was suspicious now because there were no guards at the entrance to this secret place that was the Brotherhood's.

He didn't know much about the Brotherhood. All he knew or guessed was that they were men who had banded themselves together because of their common suffering. They were men of many Arab countries who had been ill-treated by the tyrants that were many in those lands, and they had wearied of it and now they had formed this association, this Brotherhood of Tormented Men.

Tex knew that back of it all was a plan to raise the common people against the tyrants, both Arab and French, who ground down the faces of the poor and made a mockery of the word justice in these many lands. But he wasn't interested in their plans. All he wanted was the prisoner they held in this cave of salt.

They sat on their horses for many minutes, while the sun sank over the western mountains in a flood of scarlet glory that seemed to make this mountain of salt tinged with blood — an ominous appearance to the suddenly suspicious, alert little group in that winding salt valley.

They kept their eyes looking all around them, and the fact that after all this time no one came to the cave entrance and no sound was to be heard from within told them that things weren't right. All now shared that instinct for danger, which had first come to the big Texan.

Rube, the red-faced, younger legionnaire, an American of Polish ancestry, growled more to himself than to the others: 'The heck, we never figgered on this! Don't tell me the Brotherhood's gone and taken that murderin' Sturmer with them!'

But that was how it seemed to those men just then, and there was disappointment bitten like acid deep into their souls. For they had travelled far and suffered much in an effort to accomplish this mission which had carried them thousands of miles to date.

To find that Sturmer was not a prisoner here, and their search for him would have to be renewed, was more than they could contemplate equably in their tiredness at that moment.

Tex seemed to lose patience suddenly,

and he dug his heels into his horse, calling: 'Come on, let's get inside and see what happens!'

Even as he started to drive his horse forward, his sharp ears heard the jingle of bridle bits down the valley behind them.

He was still riding forward, towards that black cave mouth, but he stood in his stirrups and looked back down that shadowy white valley.

For just one instant he saw moving men, and they wore the white of desert robes, and he knew them instantly for what they were.

Tex shouted a warning, and his voice rang echoingly, breaking the silence of those curious mounded ridges of salt.

'Look out, the *partizans* are after us!'

His words seemed to electrify the group. Probably nothing else that anyone could say would have secured such swift and reckless action.

They drove their heels into the sides of their surprised beasts and sent them plunging madly, recklessly, up the slope towards the black cavern.

For the *partizans* were the dreaded

headhunters, renegade Arabs for the most part, who were employed by the French authorities to scour the desert and pick up Foreign Legion deserters and take their heads and bring them in for the reward that every deserter's head carried with it.

To find *partizans* right on their heels at this moment was suddenly terrifying. Their immediate impulse was to ride into that welcoming cave-mouth, where they could defend themselves against the superior numbers they felt sure would be in this valley-where-men-go-blind.

And yet it was not to be as they worked it out.

Tex seemed to get another hunch before he got within a dozen yards of that cave-mouth. Suddenly a thought was clamouring in his mind: 'It's a trap!'

This cave looked too innocent, suddenly, to that big, rangy Texan.

He did something then, instantly obeying his hunch, which surprised his companions and sent their horses reeling in confusion.

He fired his Lebel from his thigh, and

sent a stream of bullets ripping into the blackness of the cavern . . . for men could be back in the protective darkness and yet be able to see them out in the dying sunshine of this salt-white valley.

They could be seen and yet Tex and his companions could not see them.

But bullets could find them.

They did. There was a scream, then shouts of pain, and at once Tex knew his hunch was correct.

He shouted: 'It's a trap! They've got men inside waitin' for us!'

His horse reared and he had to fight to bring it down on all fours again, and while he was in the air he was looking back and saw the flowing robes of Arabs suddenly speeding on their horses towards them. A good dozen of them, and he caught the flash of steel and saw the lean viciousness of those professional murderers' faces as they came racing towards them.

The *partizans* were supplied with Lebel rifles, too, and they began to open up at the confused little party right there in the entrance to the cave.

That settled things for Tex. He roared: 'Into the cave!'

He knew their only chance was to dispose of the enemy lurking in the darkness of that cave, and then hold back this dozen bloodthirsty headhunters from the security that the cave offered.

He went plunging out of the sunshine into the blackness of the cave, and in a fraction of a second his eyes had adjusted to the different intensity of light.

As his horse came round, rearing because he was kicking it into these prancing manoeuvres so as to present an elusive target, he had a picture of a surprised group of Arabs reeling in confusion just within the entrance to the cavern.

They hadn't expected those snap shots. They must have been kneeling there, probably grinning to themselves in confidence as they saw the little party innocently trotting towards the trap.

But Tex's quick thinking had completely upset their plans. His bullets had found more targets than ever he could have hoped for.

Two Arabs were upon the ground still, another was writhing in agony, and probably one of the remaining two was hurt, for his gun was on the floor at his feet. Just one Arab was armed and facing them, and he was too startled by the sudden turn of events to know what to do.

Tex heard the thundering echo as his companions came galloping into that enormous, lofty cave that had been worn out of the salt mountain.

He shouted above the din of hooves stamping on bare rock: 'Down — an' keep the *partizans* back!'

Joe Ellighan, ex-Brooklyn prizefighter, and Rube Koskowsci were off their horses in an instant and running with their rifles to the cover on either side of the cave entrance. Suleiman went back and joined them, and he had a Lebel rifle that he had picked up in some desert fighting a few days earlier.

The girl didn't panic, didn't go pale with fear, but acted briskly, like a good comrade who had been blooded in battle.

She grabbed the horses and ran them

towards the sound of running water, and took them round a projecting salt column where they would be out of danger of flying bullets.

Tex came off his horse before any of the others could move, and he flung himself on top of the lone, startled *partizan*.

He crashed the man to the ground, and the rifle jarred out of the lean Arab hands, and then Tex stood up and lifted the *partizan* and shook him like a bag of old bones.

He wasn't a man to bother about the final revenge upon an enemy.

Instead, he spoke in legionnaire Arabic, which was quite well understood by the *partizan*, saying: 'Get out of here and take your pards with you. Jump to it, hombre!'

The *partizan* understood. Indeed it would have been difficult not to understand the meaning of that big, forceful legionnaire who had once been a cowboy. The Arab, his eyes nervous because he was unarmed and could not understand the meaning of the word mercy, went and picked up his companion who was writhing in pain on the rocky floor, and then he and that other Arab who had, after all, stopped one of Tex's bullets somewhere in his body, began to stumble towards the cave entrance.

Suleiman called: 'Tex, you're a fool for letting these fellows get away with their lives.'

Tex said: 'I'm a fool. So what?'

The headhunters were passing Suleiman at that moment. The hideous-faced Arab snarled: 'They should be killed. I know of no other way of dealing with people like these!'

Tex came running up, his Lebel at the ready. His face was sweating, but he didn't notice it. He just shouted: 'The hell, Sully, you let 'em get through. We don't want any more stinking corpses in this cave.'

Reluctantly Suleiman the Hideous, a man who had suffered so much that he could never forgive men who caused suffering to others, stood aside and let the trio stumble on into sunshine. Those *partizans* went uncertainly, because they couldn't believe they were being allowed to escape with their lives. They were sure they were being played with, and at any moment shots would ring out and bullets would smash through their backs.

But after a time hope came to them, and then they ran at increasing pace towards where their brother *partizans* were dismounting and running up at the crouch, their rifles ready. They reached cover in safety.

Joe Ellighan sighted, triggered, and then said: 'That guy didn't like that bullet.' Complacently he said: 'If that bullet didn't blow his brains out, it gave him a nice new partin'.'

Rube didn't say anything for a minute. Then he saw a movement, and in one swift aim and fire he brought a wild and painful yell from that incautious head-hunter. Rube said laconically: 'That fellar won't sit down for a month, I reckon.'

Tex listened to them, and then started to walk away. He knew those boys would hold the cave against five times that number of *partizans*. He went to where the girl was standing with the horses. They had waded into the underground river that flowed along a channel worn in the solid rock, and were drinking and blowing and twitching their dusty hides and manifesting every sign of equine enjoyment.

The girl turned and he saw that her face was wet and her arms were streaming with water right above the elbows, and he knew she had been drinking and drinking and drinking.

He warned: 'Don't take too much all at once or you'll blow out.'

The girl said humorously: 'That's what you always say, but I've never blown out yet. I'm going back for more.'

She knelt by the side of that lovely, cool, musically-tinkling water and began to drink again. Tex got down and drank beside her.

Then he said: 'I'll send the boys back while I keep watch.'

She looked at him in concern and said, softly: 'We're in a tight spot, aren't we?'

At that moment there was a crackle of rifle-fire at the entrance to the cave, and cordite fumes drifted back towards them and bit with acrid odour into their nostrils. Tex looked towards that patch of fading sunshine, and his eyes were sombre.

He knew it was no good trying to kid this girl. Nicky Shaw had intelligence — otherwise she would not have been picked, back in New York, for this assignment, here in the desert. She had been sent by her newspaper to investigate rumours that a former high-ranking Nazi general was serving in the French Foreign Legion, a general badly wanted by the Americans because of the atrocities he had perpetrated against their people.

She looked at him, and there was a smile on her face. It was very thin now, but to the big Texan it looked as attractive as ever. She had blue eyes, and hair bleached more than usually blonde by these days in the sunshine. She said: 'You don't need to say anything, Tex. I know how bad things are.' She gestured. 'I've seen those headhunters at work in the desert before.'

She shuddered, and then involuntarily moved closer to the big legionnaire. She gripped his arm as if she needed the comfort of his presence to wipe away the memory of that occasion when she had seen these desert manhunters leap upon a Legion deserter.

She released her hold almost immediately, smiling gallantly as Tex began to walk back to the cave entrance. Dimmy was reloading for Joe. Dimmy's shoulder wasn't quite better yet following that old wound in the desert, and it was as well for him not to go down on his face like the others and get his shoulder jarred by those vicious-kicking Lebels.

He grinned good-naturedly as Tex showed up. Tex jerked his head back towards the water and said: 'It looks safe enough back there. I reckon all our enemies are in front of us.'

He sent Joe and Dimmy to refresh themselves in the water, and then, when Joe returned, he sent Rube to drink and rest. All the time he was watching, trying to detect a movement among those folds of salt that had been deposited over countless eons of time.

Sometimes he saw movement, but it was the merest whisk of a robe or a glimpse of a bobbing headdress. It wasn't worth firing at.

But at least it let him know that their enemies were within yards of them and vigilant and watchful.

He looked up at the sky and thought: 'They're goin' to try to rush us after dark.'

It wasn't long before darkness fell. After a time the last fleeting redness went out of the sky, and suddenly there was only one shadow outside in place of the many. The whole land was shrouded in darkness, but it was a darkness that would not last, because, as Tex remembered, a small moon would be rising very soon now.

He went right back into the cave then, almost to where that smooth, running, underground river rippled away into the depths of the earth. Lying on his face, he could see the cave entrance as the faintest of silhouettes. After a time he caught a movement out there amongst the salt banks. He fired, and at the same instant rolled rapidly half a dozen yards to his right.

There was a yell from the cave entrance, which told that his shot had been successful, but instantly there was a vicious volley of rifle-fire from beyond that fallen figure. None of it hit Tex because he had rolled away from the point where his flaming rifle had betrayed his position.

Joe and Rube cracked off at some of the red points of fire out beyond the cave entrance, but probably did no damage.

Then there was silence. After a couple of hours, Tex said: 'I don't think they're goin' to try any more rushin' tactics tonight.'

That little moon was up now, and the world beyond the cave was revealed starkly in white, and with long, black shadows.

Rube was placed up at the entrance now, to watch for any swift movement out in the valley beyond, while the others grouped against the salt wall close behind him, where they would be in a position to support him if danger threatened from the *partizans*.

Nicky went off to bathe and refresh

herself while she had the opportunity. Tex got hold of Suleiman and began to talk to him.

He said: 'We all expected your friends of the Brotherhood to be here when we arrived. You for your purposes; me because your friends held Sturmer, an' I wanted him.'

Suleiman nodded, and Tex caught the movement because the big Arab's head was in silhouette against the salt-whiteness of the valley through the cave-mouth.

Tex went on: 'You were as surprised as I was, Sully, when you found your friends had gone. Now, be a pal an' tell me where you think they've gone. An' why.'

Suleiman sighed deeply, and then he said: 'There are things I should not speak of to men outside the Brotherhood, but you are a good and trustworthy comrade, Tex, so I will tell you a little of what I have been thinking these past few hours.' His eyes gleamed as they turned to look at the big Texan who had been such a good friend to the wandering Arab.

'We have come — we of the Brotherhood — from all parts of these Arab

States, determined to dispose of tyranny once and for all. As you have guessed, Tex, the Brotherhood has its men in every town and city and community throughout these vast Arab lands; in fact, everywhere where men have been tormented by tyrants of our own or alien races.

'We came to this hideout in the desert, because it was part of a plan — a plan to depose one tyrant and set up a flag of freedom under which, for the first time in centuries, the Arab *fellahin* will be able to live in security and with the knowledge that there is a justice for him as well as for wealthy despots.'

Tex revealed then his shrewd knowledge of the situation in Arab Africa. He said: 'You've got your eyes on Hejib?'

For he knew that Hejib was one of the most primitive and backward of Arab States, notorious for the brutality of its ambitious ruler, Sheik Mahmoud. Mahmoud was a man who coveted power, and even at this moment was leading an Arab army in an insurrection against the occupying French forces of North Africa.

It was a typical, fanatical Arab revolt,

but anyone with military judgment knew that it was doomed to failure from the start — because the French had modern weapons of war, whereas these Arabs were poorly equipped and badly led. But ambitious men like Sheik Mahmoud were willing to risk other people's lives if it gave them a momentary feeling of power.

Suleiman nodded. 'Yes. Hejib is the land we want to set free from the tyrants first of all. We of the Brotherhood seek to establish ourselves upon some community like Hejib, where we can demonstrate to the rest of the Arab world that men can live together and work together to their mutual advantage and prosperity. Hejib is a neglected, impoverished community, and yet with modern scientific knowledge surely the desert there could bloom as a rose!'

Tex knew what he was talking about. He had seen attempts made by European colonists to carve a living out of the encroaching desert, and he had seen them win and make beautiful, prosperous colonies in the wilderness. He agreed with Suleiman that if an attempt were made upon a scientific basis then Hejib could become a much more comfortable and prosperous place than it was at the moment under the avaricious Sheik Mahmoud.

He said: 'When does the big bang go off, Sully?' He was listening to the sounds of Nicky back there in the water. It seemed to him that she had come scrambling out of the river with unnecessary haste.

Suleiman said: 'Any day now is the time for the revolt. We picked it when we knew Sheik Mahmoud was occupied with his forces out in the desert. By now we will have brought in a hundred picked guerrilla fighters, and no doubt they will have rallied the townspeople to their side and have taken Dusa. My guess is that the Brotherhood who were hiding out in this cavern had gone to take part in the uprising.'

'And they took Captain Sturmer with them?' Tex climbed to his feet quickly. He couldn't hear any further sounds from behind him, where Nicky Shaw had been bathing in the darkness. Of course she could be standing, dressing quietly in the blackness of the cavern, listening just as he was.

But suddenly he felt uneasy and his head came round and his eyes tried to probe that velvety blackness.

At that moment Rube hissed back to them: 'I think they're gonna try another rush. Watch out back there!'

He suddenly snapped out the words, as if now he had seen a betraying movement.

But just at that moment, when Tex was about to jump for a position by the cave-mouth, a wild and frantic scream rose from the darkness behind him. It was Nicky Shaw's voice, and there was all the horror in the world in her tone.

3

Fighting For His Life

Big Legionnaire Tex whirled irresolutely. He was torn between two desires — to leap for the cave entrance, where ghostly, white-robed forms were flitting against the moonlit background of salt ridges, and to rush to the aid of blonde Nicky Shaw, screaming back there in the blackness of this mighty cavern.

There was a shattering series of sounds as the Lebels stabbed fire towards the *partizans,* who had hoped to surprise a sleeping party. At once vicious, hissing lead came gouging into the salt walls around them, and it terrified the horses, protected round that buttress of pure white crystalline deposit. They were rearing and kicking, and adding to the bedlam of sound within the echoing cavern.

Tex shouted: 'Hold 'em!' and then

leapt to where he had last heard Nicky screaming.

He ran into her in the darkness, and she must have clothed herself before she started screaming. He heard her sob, and felt her arms grip him and hold on to him and she was hysterical, and that showed the fright she had had in these last few minutes.

Tex saw nothing but blackness, and he shifted so that one arm was round that soft, shrinking form, while the other wielded the Lebel as though it were a revolver He rapped quickly: 'What happened, Nicky?'

She sobbed, terrified. 'When I was bathing . . . I began to think that someone was moving.'

'Someone was movin'?' Tex's voice was sharp. 'How could anyone be movin' back here in the cave? We saw that the cave was completely empty when we took possession of it.'

He felt that she was trembling from head to foot, and knew that she had had a terrible fright. A fresh salvo of shots came shrieking into the cave, setting up whistling echoes as they did so. The boys at the entrance leapt into action again, and their guns stammered a furious fire, and Tex knew that they were being hard-pressed.

He wanted to jump back there with them and join in this fight on which their lives depended.

But he knew he couldn't go away like that. He knew he had to stay where he was and find out if there was any truth in this story of Nicky's; because if someone was lurking at the rear of the cavern, then the defenders might be surprised and overpowered by a sudden, unexpected attack.

He could not believe it — that cavern had been completely empty before darkness fell — and there was no other entrance that he could remember, or even conceive.

Yet he had a respect for Nicky. She wasn't a fearful, imagining type of girl. Back of his mind was the thought that something concrete was responsible for her terror now.

He tried to soothe her, but his eyes

were watching alertly into the blackness around him. He said: 'It was some movement of the horses. Maybe they set up an echo an' that got you imaginin' things.'

She shook her head, and his blood seemed to chill at the decisive way in which she did it.

She said: 'I don't think I really saw anything. I don't even remember concretely hearing anything. But, Tex, you've got to believe me! When I was bathing I knew that someone or something was creeping about in this blackness!'

She was clinging to him tightly again, and now both were listening, and there was silence from the entrance to the cave, as if for a moment the *partizans* had had enough. But they heard nothing.

Nicky went on: 'I got out quickly and dressed, and I was scared all the time. But then I suddenly began to feel that whatever it was had come very close to me, and I began to turn and run towards you. I didn't want to shout, because I thought that might bring danger upon you.' Her voice was shaking again. 'I don't know what I thought. All I knew was I had to run away from this . . . *thing*!'

'Thing?' Again Tex's voice was sharp. 'Why do you keep callin' it a thing?'

She whispered: 'I don't know. All I know is I'm sure it wasn't human — whatever it was that touched me in the darkness!'

'Touched you?' Tex began to retreat at that. If something had touched Nicky, then it put an end to any theories that she had been imagining dangers. Nicky couldn't make a mistake over something touching her.

Nicky walked backwards with him, and they kept to the side wall so that they weren't a target for any sudden rifle-fire out there in the salty wastes. They were looking back into the gloom of the cavern, which was complete and unrelieved.

Nicky tried to pull herself together. 'It was a horrible moment!' she exclaimed. 'That's when I started screaming. There was something repulsive about whatever it was that reached out and touched me. The frightening thing was that it didn't seem to be altogether a hostile action!' Nicky was trying to think of words adequate to express herself, but they came with difficulty. 'The touch was almost caressing . . . as if something was examining me by touch.'

Tex said: 'By gosh, no wonder you screamed! Any time you hear me scream, you know someone's tryin' to make out what kind of a guy I am.'

He threw in that piece of terse humour in an effort to calm the girl, and he heard her laugh unsteadily and he knew she was recovering fast.

They got down behind Suleiman, and Joe Ellighan. Dimmy and Rube were crouching against the opposite wall of the cave.

Tex looked out onto a moonlit whiteness. He saw black shadows where the slanting silver rays were cut off by jagged, wind-eroded salt peaks.

Joe pointed towards the tallest peak. He said, his voice as musical as a riveting machine: 'Them guys was waitin' for that shadow to work its way round so that it covered the cave mouth. Them *partizans* thought they could slip in along the shadow, but we was ready for 'em. We gave 'em the woiks!'

Tex looked at that long, black shadow, which was moving westwards still and now the shadow was beginning to come away from the face of the cave. If the *partizans* didn't attack again within the next few minutes they would have to advance across a patch of moonlight.

So they waited, and watched that shadow slowly move away, knowing that every second that passed was in their favour. There came a time finally when a good fifty yards of moonlit space was before the cave mouth, and then they knew that the *partizans* wouldn't attack again that night.

They looked out and saw a few huddled forms, and knew that the *partizans* were suffering considerable losses in their efforts to get their heads. After this the *partizans* would attack more carefully!

Rube called across from the opposite wall: 'I guess them guys'll just camp outside until we run out of food an' have to surrender.'

That was a prospect to contemplate,

though not with equanimity. True, there was no fear of running out of water, but they had little food and would have to surrender if they weren't able to find something to eat very shortly.

No doubt the *partizans* had full water skins, and could go off and forage for food and maintain the siege.

Tex said: 'I don't intend to sit here until I'm starved into surrender.' His eyes switched to the cropped head of Suleiman the Hideous. He said: 'I'm going to Dusa in the Hejib, to try to get Sturmer again.'

The others were silent. They knew that Tex's brother had been one of the victims of ex-Nazi General Herman Sturmer, and they knew of the relentless drive within the big Texan to bring the war criminal to justice.

Joe yapped: 'What was that screamin', back there?'

Tex said: 'Nicky got scared. She thought someone was movin'.'

'What, in this cave?' Joe was frankly incredulous.

'In this cave!' retorted Nicky toughly. 'And don't you boys get to thinking that I was imagining things. I got pawed back there and I didn't like it. And you can talk as much as you like, but I'm telling you that someone or something has a back entrance into this cave.' And then she added: 'And I think there was more than one of them.'

It was disturbing information.

They sat and waited and hoped for an early dawn. After a time the moon had moved round to such an extent that its rays came slanting long and low, right to the rear of the cave; and because the walls were so white with salt, the place seemed as illuminated almost as if it were daylight.

Tex got up when he felt sure that no further attack would be made by those ferocious, lurking headhunters outside, and went carefully down to that rushing torrent of water that ran almost against the rear wall of this mighty cave.

He went carefully, alert, his finger on the trigger of his Lebel, and he went in among the patient horses and fondled them and saw that no harm had come to them. All the time he was looking everywhere for that back door that Nicky had spoken of. For in his mind was the thought that such a back door could be useful to them.

Some minutes later his companions saw the big American come walking in the moonlight towards them. He was no longer walking with any great caution, as if sure that there were no enemies to be feared at this moment.

When he reached them, lying against the wall of the cave, he grounded the butt of his Lebel and leaned on the barrel, looking down at them. By now the light was so brilliant that they could see his expression quite clearly. He looked at them for a few moments in silence, and then Ellighan yapped: 'What's eatin' you, bub?'

Tex said slowly: 'I think I've found the back door.'

That brought them on to their feet in an instant. They hadn't really believed that there could be a back door, for all Nicky's frightening experience in the earlier darkness. They crowded round him, all talking at once, until he had to raise his hand to silence them.

His tone was grimly good-humoured when he said: 'I guess we all deserve a kickin' for not realisin' it earlier.'

They didn't understand, and so he explained what had come to him belatedly.

'We should've known. When we were firin', which way did the smoke blow?'

That made them think, and then finally Rube, who was sharply observant, said: 'Why, it blew into the cavern.'

'Yeah, it blew into the cavern and not out of it,' Tex told them, and at that they began to tumble to what he was driving at. 'That means the smoke's goin' somewhere, and where smoke goes maybe we can go, too.'

By now they were all moving towards the water, until Rube remembered the ever-present danger outside and dropped back to cover the cave entrance. But the others walked down to the smooth-flowing river that was like a winding black roadway in that worn rock-channel in the floor.

Tex pointed upstream and said: 'My

guess is that that's the back door. It can't be downstream, because smoke wouldn't go that way.' He tried to explain. 'If the back door was downstream the air would, blow up and out of the cavern, but we can feel a steady draught blowing in from the wastes outside. So that means it must be ascending, and that means it must be going thataway.'

Nicky at his elbow said, softly: 'You're thinking of going thataway yourself?'

Tex nodded. His head was bent and brooding, as if weighing their chances of survival here in the cavern.

He said: 'We know what the *partizans* are like. They'll never leave this cave while they think they've got us trapped. Our heads are worth a lot of bounty money to them. In the end hunger would drive us out. So I figger we ought to try an' use this back door, if we can use it.'

There was an electrifying effect upon the party at his words. The possibility of escaping out of this deathtrap brought new life to their weary limbs. They were game for trying it — all except Nicky.

In the half-darkness where she stood in

a shadow they heard her sob a little, and at once they wheeled towards her. They heard her saying: 'I'd rather face the *partizans* than meet again that . . . *thing!*'

Tex went to her and put his arm comfortingly round her and said, soothingly: 'Honey, you sure had a fright. But this time, sweetheart, you'll have us with you an' there's nothin' you need fear.'

Nicky didn't say anything after that, and when big Tex said they must sneak away immediately, while the *partizans* were licking their wounds after that savage little skirmish of a few minutes ago, they all began to make their preparations.

They filled the skins and water bottles on their horses' backs, and they cleaned out their rifles as well as they could, and then announced themselves ready to try this back door.

The big legionnaire walked into that smooth-running, underground waterway. It came over his middle, and it was running at such a speed that he had to lean against the weight of water. The others came in behind him, pulling their horses into the water. Nicky moved up alongside big Tex and took his arm, and he knew she wasn't going to let go of him on the next part of their expedition. Only Nicky had had physical encounter with the *thing*, and so only she knew what might lie ahead of them.

Tex said: 'I figger this channel's the roadway out — if it comes out at all. So we'll walk in the darkness and follow the waterway.'

He moved out of the moonlight of that cavern, walking against the water, which plunged along its subterranean way, and within seconds they had not a vestige of light to guide them.

They were walking in the blackest of darkness, knowing their way only because they kept walking against the flowing stream.

The horses were scared at first, but then became suddenly tractable and followed docilely enough. Nicky just about bruised Tex's arm as she clung to him in horror at the thought of what could be lurking in this blackness around them.

There was little consolation in the thought that they were outwitting their enemies. For if they found no way out this way, it would mean that they would have to return and perhaps then they would find the *partizans* in occupation of the cave.

But big Tex believed what Nicky had told him — that there had been an intruder or intruders at the back of the cave. He argued to himself that where one man could go, so could another — and maybe his horse, too.

They walked on, climbing no doubt, but without noticing it in that complete darkness. They must have travelled a good mile underground, and it was quite easy and the footing underneath them was not at all treacherous. In the absence of light, the usual water-vegetation would not grow, and so the channel was free from slipperiness.

They were still in that profound and absolute blackness when all at once there was a shattering yell from Joe Ellighan.

'Somebody touched me! By jeeze, there's someb'dy down here, Tex!'

That startled shout brought them all crowding together. Joe was yapping away that something had reached out and pawed him as he passed. He was shaking from the terror of that moment, just as Nicky had been. Joe wasn't afraid of any man, but he was horrified at the thought of encountering . . . *things*.

Tex told him to shut up and listen, and they all pricked up their ears but could only hear the gurgling of water running against channelled walls. And there was still not the slightest gleam of light to guide them.

It was cool underground, but they were all sweating with fear and suspense. Suleiman spoke at length. Almost they could hear his teeth chattering. He said: 'How much farther are we going?'

Tex said grimly: 'Until we find that back door! Come on!'

Big Tex wasn't the man to give in at first fears. If that back door existed, then these underground perils had to be faced so that they could outwit those deadly headhunters.

But it wasn't pleasant, walking through

the darkness, going only against the swirling waters. All the time they expected things to reach out from the darkness and touch them — perhaps do more than touch them next time. It made their scalps prickle and gooseflesh run in shivers up and down their backs.

They went on, perhaps another quarter of a mile, and then two things happened simultaneously.

Suddenly Tex rapped back: 'I c'n see light!'

It brought joy and hope to them, and immediately they began to stumble forward faster, pulling on their horses' halters.

And then big Tex went under the water.

Tex suddenly felt something touch his shoulders, and then it seemed that hairy arms clasped round his neck, and then a great weight descended on his mighty shoulders, and, caught off his balance, he felt himself thrown head-first under the water.

In a second he found himself fighting for his life against that tremendous grip, and he knew he was being drowned deliberately . . .

4

Land of the Blind

In that powerful grip even the Texan legionnaire might have been drowned before his companions knew what was happening to him. For they couldn't see the cause of the disturbance ahead; they were in no position to help him.

They were shouting: 'What's happenin', Tex?' and their voices rose in alarm when Tex didn't speak. They were just beginning to see that faint white glow far ahead which Tex had first noticed.

Tex heard nothing of the cries of alarm from his companions. He was too madly occupied in trying to free himself from that powerful grip which kept him submerged under the smooth-flowing torrent.

Curiously, right at the moment when his lungs were bursting, and his chest was heaving as if it would split open under the strain, the legionnaire began to get an inkling of the truth . . .

Probably Tex would have been drowned within a few feet of his helpless, unseeing companions, because the attack had been so sudden and surprising, but for the fact that his horse walked on top of them in the blackness.

Tex didn't know this. All he knew was that suddenly his opponent seemed to stiffen with shock, as if something had struck him in the back.

Frenziedly Tex took advantage of that momentary relaxation around his throat. He heaved and a heavy body went splashing and sprawling in the darkness, and then Tex broke water and drew in life-giving air again. His horse reared back and he just escaped its flailing hooves, and he even felt the wind of their passage past his face.

The water was draining out of his ears and the roaring was subsiding and he began to hear the shouts of his companions.

He gasped: 'Someone jumped me! I nearly got drowned!' And then he shouted: 'Get on the inside of your hosses. Walk 'em up two by two, an' we'll walk between them!'

He didn't want to risk another assault so near to the light, which could make them the masters of this situation. He began to hurry forward again, and only after he had started did he realise he had left his Lebel rifle on the bottom of the channel. That rifle was useless for the moment, but it might mean his life if they were ever fortunate enough to reach the desert again. So he went back and fumbled and found it, and then went to the head of the little procession again and led them towards that beckoning light.

The light grew. And yet it seemed a year before they came near enough to realise what it was. They found themselves at length walking in a brightening light up this river along whose sides were ledges, which could have been pathways for nimble people. The only thing was, how could even nimble people see to keep along these precarious ledges, within that lightless subterranean tunnel, without tumbling off into the water? Yet clearly these *things* had performed that feat.

Tex's suspicions seemed to be confirmed in that moment. He thought he knew what they would meet.

They came up to that source of light and realised it was a cave much like the one they had left. It was even possible that this underground river passed through many caves in this manner, always plunging underground again. The only difference was that this cave was rock all over and without the salt walls and roof that formed that mighty cavern at the end of the valley-where-men-go-blind.

Yet when they were near enough they could see that they were still within the folds of this deposited salt — glistening, moonlit peaks of salt were revealed in the distance beyond the cavern.

They came out of the water thankfully, dragging their horses onto the stone floor of this cavern. And then, panting, they looked around them, but mostly out beyond the entrance of this cave; and they tried to imagine the terrors and dangers that lurked in that brilliant moonlight beyond. Nicky was close up against the big legionnaire, and his arm was around her because he knew she was afraid.

They stood there a long while, because Tex said it was better for them to recover from their journey and get rest. It wasn't very warm in the cave now, with their clothes wet and clinging to them, but at least they were able to recover from that struggle against the pressing river waters.

After a while Tex realised that a new peril was facing them. He had been looking out and he'd noticed the paling of the stars and the lightening of the sky and realised that dawn was at hand.

He looked at those white ridges of salt, and he remembered the ordeal of the valley-where-men-go-blind during daylight hours. Light reflecting from those white hills under this near tropical sun was sufficient to make a man go blind.

He turned to his companions and said: 'We must get out of here, pronto. We've got to get out through those salt hills before the sun is up, otherwise . . . ' He shrugged, knowing that he did not need to finish his sentence.

They all began to walk forward now towards that cave entrance — and the unknown terrors that lay beyond. But when they were at the mouth of the cave and could look out they halted in astonishment.

They were looking upon a paradise set within the folds of these surrounding salt hills. Below them was a pocket of earth surrounded by the white ridges, and careful hands had cultivated this expanse and made it a flourishing oasis.

It must have been intensively cultivated, and it suggested to Tex immediately that water from this underground river was being tapped at some other point to provide irrigation channels. He saw rectangles of vegetable gardens, and there were fruit trees and even date palms and other trees flourishing in the valley bottom. They saw houses in the distance, and they were like any other mud houses that desert Arabs built when the wanderlust was out of their bones. They were the same except for one detail, and Tex's eyes were looking for that.

They had no windows.

Tex got on to his horse and said: 'We must get out of here as quickly as possible.'

His eyes were looking towards a fold in

those salt hills, which suggested a way south out of this region of whiteness. The sun was still below the horizon but warm, red reflecting light was suffusing the morning sky. Within a quarter of an hour or so they would risk their eyes if they were caught among those brightly-reflecting salt ridges.

They all mounted and came out of that cave with a clatter of hooves. When they were out in the morning light they realised that a hundred things were crouching in a circle around this cave mouth, lurking behind boulders and any other shelter they could find, and waiting for them to emerge.

They saw them then, and knew them to be men, though they could have been . . . *things*. They were wild-looking, unkempt creatures with hair over their shoulders and beards across their chests. And not one wore a scrap of clothing.

They looked more like wild beasts than men, and they were so primitive that they had no weapons among them save for stones, which were now lifted preparatory to throwing at the invaders from the outer world.

Joe Ellighan's rifle jumped to his shoulder, but then Tex spurred across and knocked it down, shouting:

'Don't you see, *they're blind*!'

With a shock they all realised that Tex was right.

These were a people who had long lost their sight.

Perhaps they were born with sight, but living here amid the blinding light from the surrounding salt hills they had become blind, so that they were no longer affected by the appallingly severe light which came reflecting from the glittering, crystalline mass.

Tex thought: 'This is a lost world. These people and their ancestors have probably been living and cultivating this oasis for centuries. Perhaps we are the first intruders from the outside in all that time.'

But he was moving his horse in an effort to get round the flank of these people, and the others were following, holding their breaths at every sound from their harness that brought the sightless eyes of those people following them.

It was an eerie sensation, to see those

sightless men following them wherever they went. And poised in their hands were the large stones, which could have inflicted much damage on them.

Suddenly Tex put his heels to his horse and spurred, and at the same time sent it into a leap over the heads of some of the shaggy, matted-haired people. The others took their cue and came leaping after him, while the unseeing men crouched in terror at the thunderous noise, which suddenly broke out all around them.

After all it had been easy to outwit the blind!

But Tex was looking towards the east, beyond those white hills, and the light was already becoming painfully bright. There was no time to look back at those wild, naked creatures, for if they didn't get out of this oasis quickly they, too, might be blinded by the day's brilliant, reflecting sun.

The shortest way to that valley and out to the desert beyond lay through the cultivated oasis and along a track which led between the houses of this Village of the Blind.

They heard shouts of alarm from behind and guessed that the wild men were bounding after them, alarmed to hear them approach their habitations. But the horses could out-distance those blind people, and the cavalcade crashed down to where women and children were astir in the valley-bottom among the buildings.

They came unexpectedly into this little village of mud buildings, and they saw the womenfolk running indoors, clutching their children. There was terror everywhere, and yet the legionnaires and the girl and Arab had no intention of harming anyone. Suleiman even shouted it out, but it was doubtful if they even understood his language.

And then, most unexpectedly, someone deliberately ran into the road right in front of their horses. They had to halt in the narrow way between the mud buildings, because they could not run down a girl.

She was young, probably in her teens, and naked like all her people. But her long, black wavy tresses were down over her breasts, partly clothing her. And when they looked into her brown eyes they realised that here was one who had not gone blind.

They heard her speaking, but only Suleiman could understand what she was saying, and even then he gathered her meaning imperfectly.

She came running up and clutched at the bridle of one of the horses as if completely without fear of the animal, which must have been a stranger to her existence.

The light was brightening and they could see her as a lovely wild young thing, with grace in her smooth, light-brown limbs and a delicate loveliness in that little oval of a face. But it was the eyes that arrested their attention.

These weren't blind. They were big and brown and lustrous, and there was frantic appeal in them. She was begging them to take her with them — to take her away from this little land that was a world on its own.

Rube looked down at her and his face registered a mixture of emotions. He was a soft-hearted man, and it was in him at that moment to try to help this lovely girl. Then all around them there was a sudden outbreak of frenzied activity.

It was as if those womenfolk behind the windowless walls heard and understood the appeal of this girl, so different from themselves because she had sight. In an instant they were at the doors, anger making them forget a possible danger at showing themselves. A fierce clamour rose from their babbling tongues and the party on horseback knew she was being upbraided for wanting to go with them. The voices rose to a shrill cacophony of sound.

And then something crashed against a wall and shattered the dried mud and brought a small amount of debris tumbling to the ground. Those blind men had come running up, and they had heard the shrill cries of their womenfolk and were now trying to drive the intruders away. The air was filled with guttural, metallic-sounding male voices, all shouting in fury at the strangers who had come so unexpectedly upon their land.

Rube shouted: 'What'll I do, Tex?' And

his voice was desperate.

His instinct was to take the girl with him, but he knew she would be an encumbrance to their party, and they were engaged in a race against the rising sun.

Tex shouted: 'We can't take her with us! Come on, fellars!' He sent his horse plunging along the alleyway that promised to lead out to the white salt ranges, and the others began to follow, though Nicky came with reluctance.

But Tex was right in his decision. He didn't want to remain where they were, exposed to attack, and he had all the horror of a normal human being at the thought of having to resist, with force, hostile actions by blind people. Again they couldn't tarry a second longer.

The sun was already beginning to show above the hills.

Rube pulled away from the girl and sent his horse after the others, though his eyes looked back and he kept saying to himself: 'Oh, god, what a fate!' He was thinking how awful it must be to live forever in this oasis tucked in the middle of the salt mountains.

He saw the girl fall on her knees, and her head drooped as if hope had gone from her slim, vital young body. And then a woman ran out and took her by the arm and shook her, but the gesture was not unkind and Rube thought it might be the girl's mother.

Then they were settling down to the ride of their life. They rode along a trail between flamboyant trees and tall, feathery palms. On either side were the richly-cultlvated vegetable plots, and then they came out onto fields of corn that were bursting with ripeness at that time of year.

Then the soil gave way to salt as they climbed, and finally they were riding on packed white crystals that were already too bright to look at in comfort.

Tex led the way, heading as fast as he could go towards that cleft in the range, which suggested a way out onto the desert beyond. But it was over this cleft that the blazing Sahara sun was just beginning to show.

The shadows fled in a miraculously

short space of time. Almost as soon as they began to ride on salt it seemed that there was no shelter for them, and their eyes were screwed up in agony against the sharp pinpoints of light that danced up from the myriads of glistening crystals.

But Tex rode on, leading the way, and the other horses followed, though they were in discomfort. Heads down, eyes closed in agony against the intense brightness, they followed blindly that big blue-tunicked legionnaire.

How he saw his way as far as he did they never knew. But Tex rode with his eyes occasionally opening and trusting to his horse to keep to a safe footing.

But there came a time when they were not even in the neck of this pass between the salt hills, when big Tex could no longer look before him, and then he shouted in despair: 'We can't go on! I can't see where I'm goin'. I can't open my eyes any more!'

The horses halted and they all seemed to come together, their heads bowed and their eyes closed, and they were more helpless than they had ever been in their lives before. Hot waves of air came rolling across those reflecting surfaces now, and they seemed to strike them like the fiery blast from a newly-opened furnace. It seemed to make their skin shrivel and their hair to scorch, and there was a dryness over them instantly that was agony itself.

No human being could stay for more than a very short while in such an inferno.

It was at that moment when they didn't know what to do that Suleiman shouted: 'Let me get ahead. I'll get you through!'

He went riding forward, pushing his way through their horses. He had stronger eyes than their grey, Nordic ones; and he had lived most of his life in these hot desert lands. He could open his eyes a little to see where he was going, though it was agony even for Suleiman. The other horses immediately came trotting after him, and then he spurred into a reckless gallop and they felt themselves riding on level ground at last, and knew that they were halfway to safety.

Then came that glad moment when

they felt themselves descending and knew they were riding towards a desert that lay beyond. It seemed hours — years — before they could risk opening their eyes. At first the light was too much for them and they closed them quickly and rode on a little farther.

But then came a time when it was just bearable for them to look ahead, and that was because the land before them was turning into sand . . . the salt hills were running out.

The sun had just cleared the eastern horizon when they rode out of that narrow defile through the glistening white salt hills. They came onto the desert and rode for half a mile, drooping in their saddles. And then they fell out of their stirrups, bringing water skins with them, and they drank recklessly and put water on their faces and hands and even on their hair.

When this had been done and the desert breeze came to cool them they were able to sit up and look around.

Suleiman was kneeling with his head tucked among the folds of his ragged *galabier*. Tex had seen him like this once before, and knew that he had suffered agonies in order to bring them safely through those white wastes. He rose unsteadily and went over to Suleiman and bathed that hideous face, and gave him water and did all he could to comfort the man.

Suleiman tried to smile, and said: 'I'll be all right in a little while. Just let us stay here and rest.'

They sat there, looking southward away from the white mass behind them, shimmering in the ascending hot air currents that came with the heat of the morning sun. It was difficult to imagine that life existed within those folds of salt.

In time they were so far rested that they could talk. Nicky spoke at once about the girl. 'She was a lovely creature,' she said. Her eyes were wistful. 'It seems awful to think that we had to leave her in that place.'

Rube said nothing. His head was bowed under his *kepi*. He was looking at the sand and he was seeing again that sudden, startling apparition.

Tex thought about that Land of the Blind, and because there was nothing else for them to do while they rested, he speculated about them. He said: 'I reckon they've lived there for more generations than any of them can remember. My guess is they're born blind, because only the blind could survive such a white hell. But sometimes there's a freak born in every race — and in this case there was this girl we saw, who was born with good eyes and with the sense to look after them and not get herself blinded by that awful light.'

Nicky was sitting by him, her hands clasping his. To her there was no man in the world like this big, rangy Texan who had brought them through so many perils.

She said: 'I wish we could have brought her with us, Tex.'

He shrugged. 'What could we have done with her? You can't go around adoptin' gals of her age,' he said humorously, and his eyes were on the silent figure of Rube. The big Texan must have known what was going on in his comrade's mind.

Rube suddenly looked up, and there was determination in his blue eyes. He said: 'Look, you big palooka, I'll help you to get to a port with Sturmer, if ever we lay hands on the old Nazi again. But once we get him aboard a ship you know what I'm going to do?'

They looked at the fresh-faced young Polish-American and shook their heads. He said, firmly: 'I'm comin' back to that Land of the Blind, an' I'm gonna get that gal and bring her out of that hell-hole!'

Tex shrugged. He felt helpless in this situation. He knew that Rube was a good-hearted man, and he knew that he had been touched by the sight of that lovely girl alone with her good eyes in a land of blind people. He knew that if Rube set his mind on it there was nothing that would keep him from coming back and trying to rescue the girl from her appalling surroundings.

He looked at Suleiman and asked: 'You fit to ride again, Sully?'

Suleiman's ugly but good-humoured face came round and surveyed the legionnaires. His eyes were still partly closed because his head was aching from the ordeal when he had had to keep his eyes open against the glare of reflected light. He said: 'I can move now.'

So they all mounted and rode south, and rode right onto a retreating army of Arab horsemen — the army of Sheik Mahmoud, who hated the Legion more than any other man.

5

No Escape

Tex had cleaned his rifle and got it into commission again while they were resting — the action of a man who had been many years a soldier. Then they mounted and moved off and they had gone perhaps half a mile when they began to ascend a wind-dappled sand dune — one of a line of hills that stretched to the far horizon.

They were climbing, their horses' legs sinking deep into the shifting dry sand grains, when Tex's eyes saw over the summit and on to the expanse of desert beyond.

He also saw a lone rider within fifty yards of them. He was an Arab in flowing burnouse, mounted upon a milk-white racing camel. Tex saw beyond him and saw the mighty horde of Sheik Mahmoud's army at rest among the sand hills. This camel rider was evidently a scout sent to keep watch while the main force rested.

Immediately the scout threw back his hooded head and shrieked a warning. Simultaneously Tex rapped to his companions: 'Get movin'!' He wheeled his horse's head to send it plunging down that sandy slope. His startled companions obeyed without murmur, turning their horses' heads and preparing to flee.

Then the camel scout came lurching over the horizon represented by that rounded sand dune, and he was lifting his rifle to fire at them.

He did fire, and though his rifle was antiquated the shot was too close to be comfortable.

Tex reacted instinctively. His hand flashed to his belt in a lightning draw of the revolver he carried there. He did it though the Lebel was actually in his hand, but brought up on the cattle ranges of western Texas it came easier to him to throw a revolver.

The gun came out in a whirl of reflecting light. It spat flame once, and the camel rider abruptly dropped his rifle and swayed, holding his shoulder in pain. Then he turned that snaky-headed beast and disappeared out of sight.

Joe Ellighan's flat, battered face looked round and yapped cheerfully: 'That guy don't want no more fightin', I guess!'

Tex shouted: 'Goldarn it, neither do I!' He kicked his horse into best possible speed on that uncertain footing and sent them heading towards the north-east.

He was under no illusions; He knew that exchange of gunshots would bring a strong party after them from the resting army, and he wanted to have as good a lead as possible. Fortunately for them their horses were well-rested and had taken in plenty of strength-giving water in the past hours. Tex kept to the rear, and Suleiman dropped back alongside him. The big, ugly Arab had a great feeling of comradeship for this big Westerner. He never let him go far without coming to his side. They rode on, trying to keep on a straight course but having to swerve around the curving sand hills, and yet always aiming for the north-east. Within minutes they knew that pursuit was on their tracks. They heard the wild yells of Arab horsemen, and when they looked back they saw an ascending cloud of dust about half a mile to their rear. After a time they were able to distinguish the cloaked riders and the dark forms of horses that kicked up this all-enveloping haze.

The Arabs were gaining on them.

The Arabs were flogging their beasts unmercifully, all out to run down these intruders in as short a space of time as possible. But Tex knew what was behind this strategy. For slower-paced camels would be coming in the rear, so that if the Arab horses failed and went down before their riders got within rifle-range of the fleeing party, the camel squad would be coming up to carry on the pursuit.

It put the big legionnaire in a dilemma. For if he set his party to a pace as great as that of the Arab pursuers, then even if they escaped the Arab horsemen they would not have strength left to outdistance the slower-paced but longer-lasting camels.

He compromised. He and Suleiman

wheeled their horses and sighted their rifles carefully and fired and saw hooded figures roll off their horses and the rest swerve aside.

Tex and Suleiman brought their horses round at that and went racing after their companions. Twice again they repeated their tactics — when the Arab horsemen began to gain on them Tex and Suleiman turned and carefully picked off a few Bedouins and momentarily slowed the pursuit.

But this couldn't go on long, for there were at least a hundred horsemen on their tracks by now, as more and more came out from the main army in eager pursuit of the blue-uniformed wanderers.

Sweating, the dust that came up from the hooves of the horses sticking like mud to their faces, Tex and Suleiman spurred to close up with their own party. Ahead of them was a high ridge, and there was no way of detouring round it. It meant that their pace inevitably became slower as their horses sank eighteen inches deep into the loose sand, and all the while those Arabs were gaining on them.

Tex realised that they were moving now at no more than a walking pace, so he shouted to his companions to get off their horses in order to conserve their mounts' energy as much as possible. He told Nicky and the wounded Dimmy to go on ahead and lead the horses over the ridge, while the rest of them retreated, firing towards their exultant pursuers as they did so.

From this height they had a fine view over the desert. They could see the distant Arab army in that long, wide, sandy valley, and riding in column around the intervening sand hills were three files of be-robed Arab horsemen. To their south they saw a column of long-necked, long-legged camels coming at a fast pace though not moving as quickly as the horsemen.

The leading file of Arabs rode to the foot of the slope upon which they were retreating backwards, and they were firing now and they could see the white plumes of smoke and then hear the shrill whistling of lead as it flew past them, and then belatedly came the barks of rifles.

Tex squinted against the sunlight, which reflected blindingly along his rifle barrel. He sighted, triggered, and saw an Arab horse continue without its rider. He was gasping with the exertion of walking backwards on such uncertain footing, and they were all having to scramble rearwards at a mad pace.

But their only chance was to hold back those Arabs a little longer, and that meant pausing every now and then and firing down upon the converging columns below.

Rube got hit. Tex heard a sharp gasp of pain, but he couldn't turn, and he pumped more shells into the breech of the Lebel and triggered them off.

He did call, however: 'You all right, Rube?' His voice was anxious, because Rube had been a good comrade and was a great friend.

Rube said: 'I'm all right. I just lost half an ear.'

Joe Ellighan fired steadily and then, pausing to reload, yapped. 'You got another ear. Why are you complainin'?'

Rube snapped: 'When did I complain?' And he ripped off at the Arabs who were racing their mounts in a long line up the hillside within two hundred yards of them now. The air was filled with deadly, menacing lead.

They fought tenaciously, scrambling backwards and firing viciously in an effort to hold back those blood-lusting desert warriors. Rube got hit again, but again it was a flesh wound, and then Tex had a piece chipped out of his shoulder, and then both Suleiman and Joe shouted with pain as bullets tore into fleshy places. They were suffering badly now, and couldn't last more than a few seconds.

Then the horses must have gone over the ridge, and both Nicky and Dimmy knelt on top and added rifle fire to their harassed companions, struggling up the slope. It seemed to give a momentary respite to the legionnaires and Suleiman, and they turned — and raced over the ridge under the covering fire of their two companions. A wild yell of fury floated after them as the Arabs saw their quarry eluding them. Then the little party sprang onto their horses, reloading and staunching their wounds as they rode recklessly down the far slope. Nicky, her blonde hair streaming in the African sunshine, smiled gallantly round at big Tex. He heard her shout: 'We always seem to get away, don't we?'

Tex shouted grimly: 'Yeah — just!'

To his surprise he heard Nicky laugh. Then he heard her say, confidently: 'You see, we'll get away from them all right!'

He would have liked to have shared her optimism, but he was thinking of that big mob of horsemen within a few hundred yards of them on the other side of that ridge, and those long-legged camels that could overtake weary horses in a matter of hours. They didn't seem to have much chance in the long run, but he didn't say anything of this to the girl.

They went down that long, wind-ridged slope in a billowing cloud of dust, expecting every minute to hear bullets scream in among them.

Then Tex turned in the saddle just as the first of the Arabs topped that wind-swept sandy ridge behind them. For a few seconds the Bedouins were silhouetted against the blue of the African sky, their cloaks billowing out in the hot sunshine and their horses standing with heads hanging in an effort to recover from the ordeal of that climb up the hillside behind them.

Tex shouted a warning to his companions: 'Keep goin'!'

He was thinking to himself: 'Now for it!' And he rode looking back, his rifle cradled against his side ready to open fire once those Arab horsemen came plunging within range.

But those horsemen didn't stay on that ridge and didn't come down in pursuit of them. To Tex's amazement they turned and disappeared the way they had come.

Tex shouted to his companions to slow down to a walk. He was suspicious, all the same, and couldn't think that the Arabs had in fact thrown up the pursuit. At the back of his mind was the thought that those camel riders might be trying to outflank them, and this was part of Arab strategy — a pretence that the chase had been abandoned.

And yet it didn't fit somehow, and Tex looked back at the bare ridge and wondered at the abrupt departure of the Arabs. It wasn't as if they had had some sort of conference together, to decide upon such a strategy. Instead, as if suddenly all of one mind, they had turned and gone back on their tracks.

They walked their horses now to give them as much rest as possible, and they kept to the easy ways where the sand was firm underfoot and so didn't tire their overworked horses. And all the time they watched on every side of them, their rifles gripped in preparation for immediate action, looking for a movement that would tell them that those racing camels had come abreast of them.

Yet half an hour passed and there was no sign of an enemy. Then they came to another of those long sandy ridges, not as high as the one on which they had had their running battle. Again there was no convenient way of circumventing it, and this meant that they had to go across the ridge, and to help their beasts they walked and led them up.

Tex went in front, because there was no knowing what enemy lurked beyond a skyline. He held back the flapping neck curtain of his kepi as he faced the wind that blew sand in his face over the top of that ridge.

He screwed up his eyes to look around him from this height — and then he understood why the Arabs had abandoned the trail.

He found himself looking down upon another army, only this time it was the blue-coated army of France.

At once he dropped on his knees out of sight and beckoned frantically for his companions to stay where they were. Then he peered over the top of the ridge and watched that army as it tramped steadily in a north-easterly direction. Suleiman and the others came up alongside him.

Tex whispered: 'We didn't see them from the top of that ridge, but the Ay-rabs saw them. They must have thought we were a scouting party from the main army an' they pulled back when they saw they were runnin' onto the French forces.'

It had saved their lives, but it hadn't improved their position overmuch. For it meant that the little party was caught between two opposing armies.

Suleiman whispered: 'Perhaps the French have been pursuing the Arab forces ever since a battle a few days ago in the desert. But it looks as if the French have lost the trail and are going to an oasis at Khasr-el-Juba. That's just outside Hejib territory.'

Tex watched, his eyes slitted against the fierce light that was constant all over the desert. He saw mounted Spahis and coloured Colonial troops in their blue tunics and red pantaloons and blue puttees. And he saw, marching with them all, the solid ranks of France's finest fighting force, the Foreign Legion.

In all there must have been two thousand men in this expedition, and it was in fact a force formidable enough in its armament to rout the Arab Nationalist army operating under Sheik Mahmoud behind them.

But the French were plodding in a slow-rising dust cloud steadily eastwards. Perhaps they were running out of water and so had abandoned the chase of the elusive Bedouins, perhaps with the idea of resuming the fight later.

Suleiman said: 'Let us go now.' And his voice was urgent.

Tex shook his head. He didn't see any sense in moving until the French army, from which he was a deserter, passed out of sight.

But Suleiman became urgent and imperative. 'We must go, Tex. We've got to keep moving to keep ahead of Sheik Mahmoud's men.'

They all looked at the big ugly Arab who had become such a companion to them. They wanted to know why he was suddenly so insistent and so pressing. So he told them the truth.

'We must get to Dusa and warn my comrades — the Brotherhood of Tormented Men — that Sheik Mahmoud and his army are about to return to the Hejib.'

He didn't explain beyond that, but suddenly Tex made up his mind to do as Suleiman said. After all, it was in their interest to reach the coast from which they might escape out of Africa. And on the coast, if Suleiman's conjectures were correct, ex-Nazi General Herman Sturmer would be there and they might 'collect' him.

The big legionnaire from Texas rose to his feet and wiped the sweat and dust from his face, and then told them to drink and give their horses a drink and then they would take the trail again. When they had drunk sparingly from their water bottles and squirted precious fluid from the goatskins into the open mouths of their beasts, they swung into their saddles, not without some groans and protests from the wounded Joe and Rube.

But no one was badly hurt, and they began to strike due east, keeping always to the low ground in an effort to evade detection by the armies lying parallel to them on either side.

When night fell Suleiman asked them to keep going. They had to get ahead of the Arab army, and only a forced night march would enable them to do that. Tex compromised, and they had two hours' rest; and then, when the moon was up and lighting their way, they got into their saddles and rode wearily eastwards again.

A day and a half later a lookout man on the tower of the fortress-palace of Sheik Mahmoud saw a small party approaching from the west. What excited him, though, was the fact that most of them wore the hated blue of the legionnaires' uniform. His shout brought the Brotherhood — those leaders of this revolt of the fellahin against their masters — out on newly-acquired horses to meet the advancing party in the desert.

Tex and his companions saw them bearing down on them, a thunderous mob of advancing horsemen, and they closed together and their rifles came up under their arms, ready for action if it were necessary.

But Suleiman rode forward, his hands raised aloft to show they were empty of weapons, and the approaching Arabs must have recognised him and they circled round him, while the legionnaires sat back on their horses and awaited the result of the conference.

After a few seconds Suleiman signalled to them to approach, and Tex kicked his heels into his horse's sides and led the way towards that ragged group of Arab horsemen. But he called to his companions: 'I don't care what promises they make, I don't give up my rifle!'

He heard the growling voices of the other legionnaires — 'Neither will we!'

The reception that those Arabs gave the legionnaires was mixed. There were some who found it in their hearts to be able to smile upon these men who had helped one of the Brotherhood. But most could only look at that blue uniform and hate all who wore it.

For many had suffered under the rigours of French occupation.

Nicky rode alongside Tex, for she was uneasy at the sight of so many ferocious-looking, unprepossessing men around them. Big Tex leaned across and took her hand and said softly: 'We'll be all right. Sully's rootin' for us!'

So it seemed. For the Brotherhood formed into a procession behind the weary little party, and they came in some sort of triumph, almost, to where hundreds of Arabs lined the walls of the fortress-palace that had been wrested from Sheik Mahmoud in his absence.

Wearily they alighted in a Courtyard that was inviting because of the fountains that played in cooling, lily-covered ponds, and where there was shade from tall palm trees and the scent of lovely Arab roses to please them. At once someone came down to them and said something to Suleiman, and then they were led into the palace itself.

They didn't know where they were going, or why. But they were content to follow behind Suleiman and the guide through ornate reception rooms of the palace until suddenly they were shown into the mighty banqueting hall, the scene of all great function's here in the Palace of Dusa.

It was a spacious hall, with carved supports to beams that hung across the void high above their heads. The walls had been painted and decorated by skilled Arab artists, and there was a wealth of luxury in the ornamentations — those few that had escaped the pillaging hands of the looters.

Right at the end of this great hall was a dais, and on it, framed against a background of coloured silken drapes, reclining upon multi-coloured cushions, was a young girl.

When they saw her, their eyes grew wide in wonder. They halted where they were, for each thought they recognised her.

And then suddenly Suleiman went plunging forward, and a name was on his lips and his hands were out-stretched in welcome. They heard him say incredulously: 'Mahfra!' and then they knew they had made no mistake.

This was Mahfra, a peasant girl whom they had picked up in the desert in an earlier adventure. Now they gazed at her in astonishment, for she was like a queen there among those soft, luxurious cushions.

Suleiman halted after his first few involuntary paces. Tex looked quickly at him, and he saw the light shine in those big, brown, good-tempered eyes of this awfully ugly man. He had pity in his heart for Suleiman then, for he knew that Suleiman was in love with this girl, and he felt that no girl could ever love a man whose face had been twisted by torture into this grotesque shape.

But Mahfra was no queen by nature, and these were her friends, and she rose from those cushions gladly and came running towards them, her arms outstretched in greeting. And it seemed to Tex that her gladness embraced even the tall Suleiman.

In a moment they were all crowding round her and admiring her silk robes and the jewelled diadem that encircled her rich dark tresses. Almost incoherent in her gladness she told them how she had been set up as the queen of the Hejib — a gesture designed to annoy the aristocratic Sheik Mahmoud when he heard that one of low birth sat on the throne of his country.

Tex shared in the gladness of their meeting, but he was a man who had been made wary by the circumstances of his hard and dangerous life, and he was looking beyond this attractive Arab girl as she chatted to his crowding companions. He was looking to where a sullen but lovely Arab girl stood like a handmaiden over where Mahfra had been lying, and he wondered at it.

He was not to know that this was a punishment meted out to the spoilt and pampered daughter of the absent sheik. That it was the Greek's idea that the great should know what it felt like to be a servant of others.

Tex's eyes moved round the room to where a tall handsome young man stood quietly awaiting their attention. He recognised him at once as the leader of this Brotherhood, whom he had met before. He looked at that fine Greek countenance that was yet pure Arab and he met the calmness of those eyes and was conscious again of the princely dignity of the Tormented Man's bearing.

In that same instant he had a sense of danger. For he knew that this man was inflexible in his determination. He knew that he was ruthless in the pursuit of his desires, and though those desires were laudable — the betterment of the oppressed in these Arab lands — there were times when the Greek went back on his word and compromised with promises he had made.

Tex's eyes narrowed, because he had a feeling there was calculation in the Greek's eyes as they watched the group of legionnaires.

He began to walk across to him. He was a few paces away from the leader of the Brotherhood when he heard sounds of drilling, out in the back regions of the palace. His head turned and he looked through a high un-shuttered window.

He saw a scrub-covered wasteland, and on it were groups of ragged Arabs — those citizens of Dusa who had rallied to the flag of freedom set up by the Brotherhood here in Hejib.

Then he saw that one squad was being drilled by a man who wore the blue uniform of an officer of the Foreign Legion, and yet wore the kafir headdress of the desert nomad.

Big Tex's fists clenched and his eyes blazed, for he knew that man out there. This was Herman Sturmer, the Nazi general who had sought anonymity in the ranks of the French Foreign Legion. This was the man who had killed a thousand American soldier-prisoners — and one of them his brother!

Tex began to go towards that window, for this was the prize that he had come tens of thousands of miles to capture. Here was the criminal wanted by the Allied War Crimes Commission, and they were out of French territory, and there was the harbour and the possibility of getting Herman Sturmer out of Africa.

A cool voice called to him: 'One moment, *mon legionnaire.*'

Tex swung round. He looked into the eyes of the Greek. His hand gripped the Lebel the tighter, but he turned and went towards the leader of this insurrection.

Those two big men faced each other in that great ceremonial hall. Then Tex spoke, and his voice was grating: 'I want that man out there!'

The Greek smiled and said softly: 'We need that man more than you, legionnaire.'

Tex felt the anger rising in him, because he knew that the Greek was master of the situation, and after all they had gone through it was infuriating to be in this situation.

He said: 'I'm goin' to take him away.'

The Greek shook his head, a smile of amusement on his handsome face. 'You'll take him away when it suits us,' he said. Then his eyes seemed to go hard. His head lifted and he said, almost peremptorily: 'And I need you and your companions, too, at this moment.'

Tex realised that Suleiman had come quietly up to his side and was listening. The Greek's eyes looked at Suleiman the Hideous, and a smile of pleasure came to them, and the two clasped hands, Arab fashion, in greeting. The Greek bade his comrade welcome.

Suleiman gave him the news immediately. 'Sheik Mahmoud and his army are heading for Dusa,' he said urgently. 'We must be ready when he comes.'

The Greek merely smiled confidently. 'We were careful to permit the sheik's cousin to escape from us and so ride out and tell Mahmoud that he had lost his country to an uprising of beggars. We knew we could then expect Sheik Mahmoud to return with his defeated army — defeated by the French he sought to throw out of Africa — and we have been preparing for him.'

His eyes were back on Tex now.

He said: 'I was just making additional plans for our defence.'

Tex swung round angrily upon Suleiman: 'Look, Sully, you know I came to Africa to get Sturmer. Well, he's out there right now.' He nodded towards the wasteland where Sturmer was drilling the Arabs. 'I want to take him away, an' I intend to take him.'

Suleiman put his hand on his friend's faded blue tunic. He looked into that brown, perspiring, angry face and he smiled tolerantly. 'I know how you feel, Tex. I would like to help you, but I cannot. We need people like Sturmer to teach the people how to use arms to defend themselves when they try to take this town away from us.'

Suleiman shrugged expressively.

'What do you think would happen if we allowed Sheik Mahmoud to win?' he asked. His voice was cynical. 'There would be slaughter such as this coast has rarely known. There would be the torture of men on a scale to surpass anything in

Mahmoud's life to date. No, Tex, too many people have too much at stake for us to hand over a man as valuable as Sturmer for you to take away from us.'

The Greek came into the conversation then. He said, amusement showing in his voice: 'That is just what I was explaining to our American friend. Sturmer is working well for us and he is training men in the use of the arms we captured from the palace armoury. Even more important, he is teaching Arabs an unaccustomed form of warfare — battle from trenches.'

The Greek turned now so that he smiled fully upon the tall, fuming American. 'Perhaps you did not notice as you came in that already the land for a mile out beyond the town has been trenched, so that our defenders of freedom can surprise Sheik Mahmoud when he comes charging in with his cavalry?'

Tex knew he was beaten. More, he realised that he couldn't expect these Arabs voluntarily to turn over to him a military expert in desert warfare like ex-Nazi General Sturmer.

Then the Greek continued softly: 'You,

Tex, and your friends can train men along with Sturmer. And when the attack comes you can go in the trenches along with my men and help to stiffen their resistance.'

Tex's eyes flamed with anger. 'This isn't my war,' he bit off. 'I'm tired of fightin' an' I don't intend to do any more.'

The Greek said: 'What do you intend to do?'

Tex looked at the Greek and spoke outright. He said: 'I intend to get the hell out of this place just as fast as I can make it!' Then his jaw thrust forward belligerently. 'An' I intend to take Sturmer with me if I get a chance!'

The Greek said: 'I don't think you're going to get much chance, Legionnaire Tex.' Saying that he gestured, his hand seeming to embrace the entire room.

Tex turned.

He saw that every doorway — and there were many leading out of that big ceremonial hall — was solid with silent staring brethren of this association of Tormented Men.

And he knew there was going to be no escape from them.

6

'You're Not Going Back!'

Tex heard the gasp of alarm that came from Nicky, and then all in one moment those four bandaged, bloodstained legionnaires were grouped about Nicky and Mahfra, their rifles pointing and covering them on every side.

Yet those crowding, silent men in those many doorways never moved towards them. There was not even a weapon visible. But the effect of their presence was sufficient.

There was a threat in that menacing throng, and Tex knew that the Greek had planned it this way. This man they called the Greek was planning shrewdly and boldly. He was using an officer of the Foreign Legion to train his ragged forces, and now he was determined to make these four legionnaires assist also.

The Greek smiled, though he was

within a couple of yards of those legionnaires' rifles. He was a man without fear, apparently.

He said, softly: 'What is your answer now, legionnaire?'

Tex met the eyes of his companions, lingering last of all on the blue ones of the newspaperwoman from New York. Then he looked at the Arabs surrounding them and he knew he could give only one answer if their lives were to be spared.

He said, gratingly: 'Okay, brother, you win. We'll train your bozos, an' we'll try an' whip 'em into shape to meet Mahmoud's forces. But I'm tellin' you somethin' right off the record.'

The Greek looked interested. He inclined his head as if to solicit the desired information, but he didn't speak.

Tex went on: 'Brother, you don't stand a cat in hell's chance of licking Mahmoud an' his army!' His hand waved to the tattered mob in the doorways. 'Don't think I'm out of sympathy with you when I say that, but I know men an' I know Arab fightin' men especially. These men you've got followin' you are desperate enough at this moment. An' they're ready to learn an' shoulder rifles. But what's goin' to happen the moment they see Mahmoud's cavalary crashing down on them in their trenches?'

His voice was hard as he shot the question at the Greek. The smile had left that handsome face now, and there was the coldest of calculation in those eyes.

'What will happen?' the Greek softly asked.

Tex shoved his head forward as if to add weight to his words. 'They'll throw down their rifles an' get the hell out of the way,' he said. 'You've got broken men followin' you, Greek. All their lives they've been kicked around and done as they're told an' most of 'em won't forget the habit of years, an' when Sheik Mahmoud comes riding up with his hundreds of horsemen — all trained fighters — they'll lose heart and turn and desert you.'

The smile was back on the Greek's lips now. He was genuinely amused. 'They won't do anything of the sort, American,' he smiled. 'I know men, and I know that those who follow the flag of the diagonal cross will fight to the end. They have suffered all they are prepared to suffer, and now they are thirsting to be revenged on the tyrant.'

Some of that audience around those doorways must have understood the language in which those words were spoken, for there was a murmur that swelled as voices rapidly interpreted. The insurgents plainly believed the words of their leader. At this moment they had all the valour in the world.

Tex shrugged. 'Sure, I know how they feel. We all feel like that until we hear the sound of bullets whizzin' by an' then we start to get wise an' think second thoughts. I'm still prepared to bet that no matter how much we train your men in trench warfare — an' we've only got a matter of a coupla days,' he said cynically, ' — when the time comes you'll find a lot skedaddling and lettin' the tribesmen come in with their guns and swords.'

He grounded the butt of his Lebel. His thoughts weren't pleasant. He was think-ing that the alternatives before them amounted to the same thing. If they refused to help the Greek in the training of this rabble, they wouldn't go on living, that was pretty plain to him.

And if they did stay and try to help these insurgents, there wasn't much doubt that Sheik Mahmoud's vengeful forces would break through and cut them all to bits, legionnaires included. Maybe, he thought grimly, they might have a slower, more painful end, than just being hacked down in the field of battle. Mahmoud would be mighty sore about these happenings behind his back!

The Greek turned away then, as if he was satisfied with things. Tex watched him with brooding eyes that were yet admiring as they saw the fine, patrician-looking man in tattered robes walk in dignity out of the ceremonial hall. He felt sure that this man's plans had over-reached themselves, and he was riding for a fall. But there was no doubt about it, the man was a fighter through and through, a man after his own heart!

Someone came out from among the crowd, and spoke rapidly to Suleiman and then started to go out of the room. The crowd in the doorways began to drift away. Suleiman beckoned to his companions and said: 'Come on, friends. We've got some rooms placed at our disposal. We have three hours' rest and then we must come out and help Sturmer drill the men.'

Tex could have groaned at the hopelessness of the situation. They couldn't make fighting men of these people in a matter of hours! Grudgingly he conceded that they could be taught to load and aim and fire a rifle, and that was something. But it wasn't much good teaching a man to fire a rifle if a soldier's spirit wasn't at the same time inculcated, so that he did not throw away that rifle at the first sign of danger and run for safety.

They went up into three balconied rooms that had been set out for them. Mahfra came up with her friends, for she didn't like this pageantry of the Greek's, who had insisted upon the rigmarole of making her queen of the Hejib. She was a peasant girl, overawed by circumstances, and wanted nothing more than to be with people she trusted.

Tex had to grin as he saw the dusty, trail-stained American girl link arms with the 'queen' of the Hejib and retire into a room that had been placed at her disposal.

The men all went into a cool, shady room that faced north and so avoided the hot rays of the sun. They lowered themselves onto cushions that had been left for them and threw off as much of their clothing as they could. And then they lay and looked at each other through the grime on their faces until Rube said, hollowly: 'Now what?'

Tex looked at Suleiman, and said: 'I'm trustin' you, Sully.'

Suleiman looked unhappily at the legionnaires, and then said: 'Look, you've got to know how I stand. My heart is with this revolt. I am pledged to help it even at the cost of my life and I'll do that. But when I hear you, Tex, say so positively that we'll never hold this place against Sheik Mahmoud's forces, it makes me want to do other things than just stop here and die.'

He got to his feet then in his unrest, a big raw-boned figure, incongruous in his long, tattered *galabier*, and with the knitted skull cap on his ugly head.

But he was a man and a fine man for all his appearance, and the legionnaires had a respect for their companion.

Suleiman continued passionately: 'There's so much suffering in these lands, and I've wanted all my life to do something to free the people, and this project of the Brotherhood seemed a beginning. If we could win Hejib and make it an independent state where men were truly free of tyrants and where justice could be installed, then I would give my life. But there are so many other things that a man wants.'

Tex told him one of them. He said, gently: 'You are in love with Mahfra, aren't you? You'd like to have a wife, an' Mahfra is the girl of your choice. Before you met her you didn't care if you did die. But now you want to live because you want to win her. Isn't that it?'

The other legionnaires looked quickly, curiously, at the big scarecrow of an Arab, at this man with the revoltingly ugly face.

They hadn't suspected what lay in Suleiman's breast, but Tex had known it for a long while.

Suleiman turned in an effort to avoid their eyes, and tried bluster. 'You're talking crazy, Tex,' he told him. 'I mean, look at me. Look at the face that men gave me in the torture cells at the Citadel, and then ask yourself what chance have I got of ever getting a girl to be my wife!'

Tex was thinking — hard. He said, slowly: 'I started to talk to you about this once before. I've got plenty of money back in the States, an' I'll pay for the finest plastic surgeon in America to give you a face that'll make even the Greek envious. When the surgeon's through with you, Mahfra will be glad to have you.'

Now it was Tex's turn to rise. He spoke on, and his voice was very soft, so that only Suleiman understood his words.

'You don't know it, Sully, but Mahfra kinda likes you as it is. Oh, I know you make her shudder and turn away when you get too near with that pan of yours, but she can feel the kind of man you are underneath and she likes you.'

Suleiman's big brown eyes seemed to be hanging onto Tex with a kind of desperate longing. As if he wanted to believe what was being said to him, but didn't dare. 'You can't mean this, Tex!'

'I do mean it, Sully,' the former cattleman answered. 'Now, let's make a pact, shall we? We'll get out of this town as quickly as we can, an' when we go we'll take our man with us — General Sturmer.'

He had moved across to the window and was looking down at that ship in the harbour. A wisp of white vapour was coming from a valve by the siren. It suggested that steam was being maintained aboard.

Tex said: 'We'll get away in that ship. I reckon that Rube can manage any engines ever made, an' we'll get away aboard that hulk somehow.'

Tex's thoughts were flitting down these avenues of escape. Desperate men could achieve anything, and getting away aboard that ship didn't seem to amount to any great hazard. The thing was to appear to play ball with the Greek, then slide off when the opportunity presented.

He came away from the window and then he realised that Suleiman was standing there and the big Arab was very silent. Tex said: 'What's on your mind?'

Suleiman looked at him, and there was an agony of longing in his eyes. For once in his life there was an easy pathway open to him. Yet he shook that big ugly head of his that kept him apart from most men except the Brotherhood. He said: 'I can't do that, Tex. These are my friends and I am committed to this venture. Not for a new face — not even for Mahfra — would I walk out on them now.'

A little warm light kindled in Tex's eyes. He said: 'I think I understand. And I think I like you the better for the decision you have made.' It was different for the legionnaires who were not morally committed to this enterprise. Tex looked down at the tiled flooring that was so cool even now in the heat of summer, and then said, slowly: 'Maybe I'll have a proposition to change your mind soon, Sully.'

He was an obstinate man, this American, and in his heart he was determined that Suleiman, who had been such a fine comrade, should have a chance of a new life.

When he went away from Dusa he was determined that Suleiman should go with him. Already his brain was flitting through the possibilities of a plan that had suddenly flamed in his mind.

Suleiman didn't get excited, though he had a respect for this big American's planning. He said: 'Let me tell you one thing more, Tex. I'm giving you this warning in all friendliness. It doesn't matter what promises are made to you in the future, you and your friends are bound to die. Too many of the Greek's followers hate men who wear your uniform. They will never allow you to get out of this country alive.'

Tex looked down at his companions and a grin came to his face. He said, with a cheerfulness that surprised them all: 'This looks like the biggest jam we have ever been in, doesn't it, boys?'

Yet they knew by the way he said it that he was not without hope, that in fact he was confident he could defeat all these enemies who planned their death. He wouldn't say more, and he got down again to rest, and Nicky came and joined the men because she felt lonely away from her companions, and even Mahfra came in to them. Suleiman kept watching Mahfra, and Tex saw that the Arab girl in her lovely new finery kept stealing little glances across the room to where the big Arab lay stretched alongside a wall.

Two hours later they stirred themselves and went down and found water and washed away the dust of the trail and some of the fatigue that was still upon them. And then a group of Brothers came with orders from the Greek that they should go out to help Sturmer issue rifles and ammunition, and instruct Arab peasants in the use of them.

They went out into the sunshine that was still too hot to be comfortable, though in two hours or so the sun would have set. Sturmer was out there with a squad of twenty ragged men from the gutters. They were all excited and cheerful, but presented a spectacle that was, to say the least of it, unmilitary. Sturmer was displaying unusual patience in handling them. Perhaps he wasn't bothered if they didn't absorb their lessons anyway.

Tex and his companions were led across towards Sturmer by the Arabs, and Sturmer turned to look at them as they came over, their Lebels gripped in their hands.

They saw that well-remembered face — a face that had been pictured in American papers so many times as a man wanted for crimes against the American people. It was a thin face, utterly unlike that expected of a soldier. He looked like some rather insignificant, harmless clerk, but they knew his record, and it was written in blood and this was no clerk but a monster.

They caught the glint of light reflecting on those prissy, rimless glasses, which added to his clerkish appearance, and it seemed almost as if his eyes were glowing with satisfaction. He waited for them to approach.

When they were five yards away, Tex and his legionnaires halted. Sturmer looked at them arrogantly, with all the old contempt of a Nazi general for his subordinates.

Then Sturmer's thin, metallic voice clipped out words — 'You are reporting to me for duty. I am your superior officer and what I tell you has to be obeyed. You understand that, don't you?'

Those American legionnaires leaned on their rifles and looked at him, and no word was spoken between them.

The Arab brethren joined in at this and shouted, as excited Arabs always do, that the legionnaires had to obey this officer. They didn't know the background to the relationship between these legionnaires and a man of higher rank in the French Foreign Legion. They thought that the legionnaires were being obstinate and awkward, and that it was in fact a good plan to put them under the charge of this officer.

Sturmer reacted according to type. He seemed to swell out with anger because they stood and looked at him and didn't answer his question. He shouted at them: 'You dogs, why don't you speak? I will have the hides off your backs if you aren't co-operative!'

He thought he was back in the Legion again, where men leapt to obey the order of a superior officer, because not to obey could bring the most frightful punishment upon them.

Still these legionnaires never moved, and never took their eyes away from him. They leaned on their rifles and just looked at him and waited for him to begin something.

He did.

He was too sure of himself, and too anxious to repay old scores. He came jumping forward, determined to make them do his will.

He was shouting to them to stand up straight, to stand to attention like soldiers, and in future they would salute him, or *mein Gott*, they would be for it!

To emphasise his point and to show them that he meant business, he took a swipe at Tex, who happened to be in the lead of the party. He didn't connect. Tex ducked and that swinging fist swept over the top of his *kepi*.

Tex straightened after the blow was delivered, and they heard him sigh like a man whose patience has become exhausted. He never said a word but handed his rifle to Rube to hold. Then he went forward and before that fuming, arrogant officer knew what was happening to him, big Tex had picked him up by the ears and tossed him a dozen yards away into the dust.

There was a howl of laughter from Sturmer's ragged squad. It tickled their Arab sense of humour to see one of the great humbled in this manner. So Sturmer tried to save his face — he knew that he had lost his power to command if he took this lying down.

Mouthing ferocious German oaths Sturmer came leaping in with fists and feet flying. He tried to batter his way through Tex's defences, but Tex kept going back, retreating, and thus evading the full force of those savage blows. And Tex's eyes were grim and grey and narrowed.

He let Sturmer come rushing in again, and then he got one arm crooked between Sturmer's legs and the other big hand clasped behind the ex-Nazi's neck, and Sturmer was lifted off his feet like a child and then tossed on his back once again in the dust. This time he didn't get up in any bellicose mood. This time he stayed on the ground for about half a minute, hardly moving, and then he picked himself up, and walked slowly, painfully, away.

That was a Nazi general who would never again try the high-hand on those Americans.

It produced consternation among the Brothers. They began to shout at each other and to argue, and one ran after Sturmer but was shaken off; then they came back and jabbered at the legionnaires, so that they found themselves surrounded by scrub-faced men with an assortment of skull caps and turbans and *kafirs*, in robes that were of many colours but consistent only in their raggedness.

Tex said: 'Okay, okay!' He lifted his hands for silence and then went on: 'Just leave your boys to us. We'll finish Sturmer's work, but it won't do you any good in the long run.'

For the next two hours, apathetically

they instructed eager but unpractised Arabs in the art of loading and firing an assortment of guns, many of which weren't safe to be used because of their age and condition. Still, this was the Greek's orders and they were following them.

When dusk came they all went back into the place where food had been laid out for them. They were tired men wanting a night's sleep, and yet there was so much for them to talk about and think about before they allowed themselves to rest. For they knew that Sheik Mahmoud couldn't be very far away in the desert. Only their forced night marches had placed them ahead of the Arab army.

Nicky sat with the men, and Suleiman came up and joined them, though he told them that the Greek did not like to see him fraternising with legionnaires as he did.

'But I don't desert my friends,' Suleiman told them shortly, and they guessed at that that Suleiman had had a row with the Greek over this friendship.

Tex looked at Suleiman and said; 'I've made my plans, Sully.'

That interested them all, Nicky included. She put down her precious camera that she had managed to bring through all her perils with her, and looked anxiously at big Tex.

Tex said: 'We're goin' out on that old hulk down there. We're goin' with clear consciences, and that'll include you, too, Suleiman.'

Suleiman's eyes were eager but he held in his excitement. He said: 'I can only go with you if I have done my share here and helped to defeat Sheik Mahmoud.'

'You'll have a clear conscience,' Tex promised grimly. At that everyone came crowding closer, wanting to know what Tex had in mind.

The sun was a blood-red glow on the western horizon, and in the coolness of the courtyard under their window the excited talk of Arabs rose to their ears.

Tex said: 'Listen to them! They've got all the guts in the world now, but they don't stand a chance when Mahmoud comes ridin' through with his Arab cavalry. But I've got a plan an' I think it'll work.

'I'm goin' to that Greek to tell him that

147

I can fetch that French army to his aid. This land of Hejib has changed rulers, don't forget. Mahmoud is no longer the ruler of this province, and if the new government — or whatever they like to call themselves — care to invite French troops into Hejib territory to clear out Mahmoud, then they can do it without causing international complications. The French would love an excuse to come in after Mahmoud and his men, instead of having to try to do things through United Nations' courts.'

They listened to him, but there wasn't an immediate reaction of enthusiasm. Nicky's first thought was of Tex. She shook her head vigorously, and said: 'You're not going back to the French Foreign Legion, Tex! You're a deserter, though perhaps they don't know it yet. But it won't be easy to get away from the French Foreign Legion a second time.'

Tex lifted his hands in protest. 'Okay, okay. So what do we do? Sit here an' get ourselves hacked to bits because that Greek thinks his inspired rabble can hold a trained desert army?'

He stalked across the room, and there was finality in his movements.

'Like hell I'm goin' to sit around and wait for that kind of fate!' he said grimly. 'Mahmoud will be showin' up any time now, an' I'm going right down to that Greek to tell him what's in my mind. If you don't see me again you'll know he's given me a horse and I'm on my way to find the French.'

That was all he said as he strode from that room, big and rangy and very confident in himself. That was just like Tex; the moment he got an idea he was prepared to back it with all he'd got. Just now it seemed to him, in any event, that the alternatives warranted the risk of going back to the French Foreign Legion to enlist their aid.

There was no ceremonial leave-taking, though. Nicky looked as if she was going to weep when the door closed on Tex. They all sat there and talked in desultory fashion until the light failed and darkness grew. They were listening for the sound of hoofbeats that might tell of the big legionnaire's departure, but they heard none.

Rube at length stirred himself and became brisk in his manner. He said: 'We'll be training those boys tomorrow — unless Mahmoud shows up, and then we all go into those trenches and try to hold him back. But if we get a chance I reckon we should get down to that ship in the harbour and see what's needed to take her out to sea.'

He was beginning to enlarge upon the possibilities of escape, becoming enthusiastic, as was his way.

Then the door opened slowly, and a man walked in. It was Tex.

He said: 'The Greek says he doesn't need French assistance.' They could hardly see his face in that darkness but they knew there was bitterness on it. 'Sully, your chief's just condemned you an' us an' all the people who have dared to take up arms against Mahmoud!'

7

'Where's Tex?'

The Greek had been in that ceremonial room, when Tex went in search of him. He was squatting cross-legged among the cushions where Mahfra had been sitting earlier that day, and with him was a tattered crew of Brothers — his 'cabinet'.

Tex had settled down among them, in Arab fashion. The Greek had looked at him in that calm, rather god-like manner of his. In time, in the way of these courteous Arab people, the stranger had been invited to speak.

Tex had been blunt.

'You don't stand a chance when Mahmoud rides in with his cavalry.' He was emphatic on the point in a manner that brooked no denial. 'You might beat back the first attacks, but in the end Mahmoud will overrun you and will put you all to the sword — if he doesn't hang you instead!'

The Greek merely nodded politely. 'You have said all that before, O Legionnaire.'

'But I'm sayin' more than that now.' Tex's grey eyes looked from one fierce, hungry face to another. 'I'm goin' to tell you how you can lick Mahmoud an' keep this place as you desire.

'Not more than a day's ride from here is the oasis, Khasr-el-Juba. I guess that the French forces that have been warring with Mahmoud's army are resting up there. I could go to them and get them to come after Mahmoud and catch him in the rear when he's busy tryin' to capture Dusa.

'The French could enter Hejib territory by invitation, and you, as present ruler of this province, can extend such an invitation. There isn't any time to lose. You'd better make your minds up quickly, because it's a long way to Juba, and the French will take even longer to get into the Hejib.'

When he had finished he looked round at those faces, and then the Arabs began to speak among themselves in the many dialects of Arabic. Only the Greek didn't speak, but squatted there cross-legged, his calm, brown eyes resting on the big legionnaire's face.

In time it seemed that the Greek grew impatient with the altercation around him, for he lifted his hand for silence, and then, without consultation with his Brothers, he announced the verdict.

'We do not need French assistance. We will not seek the aid of one tyrant to defeat another. The hearts of our liberated people are strong, and we shall defeat Mahmoud in battle, and if the French come into the Hejib, we shall defeat them too.'

It was the voice of a man who had become a little arrogant because of the ease with which his plans had matured. Like many another leader before him he was losing his sense of proportion.

The Arabs with the Greek nodded vigorously and gave voice to approving of the decision. They spoke gutturally, in quick angry sentences, and their eyes were hostile and unfriendly as they looked at the legionnaire.

In time Tex realised what they were getting at.

They thought this a cunning trick on his part to bring French troops in to take over Hejib territory. They did not trust any man who wore the blue of the Foreign Legion.

With such suspicion and bitterness opposed to him, there was nothing to be gained by staying and arguing with them. So Tex rose reluctantly, making a gesture with his hands as if to dissociate himself from the decision made.

He merely said: 'You're signin' your own death warrants. I've given you a chance, but you won't take it. Wal, I guess there's nothin' else for me but to go an' have a good night's sleep before Mahmoud comes to shoot the life out of me!'

He walked out of the conference at that, but he heard the angry voices that rose at his departure, and he knew that whatever happened — whoever won this coming battle for Dusa — the legionnaires would never get out of the territory alive. These Brothers, all except Suleiman, hated all invaders of African soil.

They would kill them when they no longer needed them — that is, if the forces of Mahmoud in some mysterious way failed to squash this revolt in the Hejib.

When he had given the Greek's decision to his companions, Tex was as good as his word, and simply announced that he was going to sleep, which he did. He lay down on the soft cushions which furnished this lovely room, and in a few moments he was fast asleep.

Next day they were out early before the heat of the sun was fully upon Dusa, with hundreds more of the fellahin to instruct in the use of arms which were being brought from Mahmoud's armoury. The peasants were excited by their weapons, but they weren't to realise that these were of old and indifferent quality, which was why they had been left in the armoury. Mahmoud's desert fighters had been supplied with much more modern, up-to-date weapons, most of them salvaged from the desert fighting when Rommel and Montgomery were warring in Africa.

The guns ran out before noon and the instruction in their use was very perfunctory in any event. After which the Greek ordered the legionnaires, including Sturmer, to instruct the armed men in trench warfare. Trenches had been dug all around the perimeter of the town, though in most cases the soil had been thrown the wrong way.

It was all so unreal that many times the legionnaires looked at each other helplessly, and then burst out laughing. It was fantastic to think that anyone could suppose that in a matter of hours, untrained, undisciplined men could be welded into a fighting force as the Greek seemed to expect.

There was nothing else for it, however, and the legionnaires did all they could to instruct their troops. Not one had any idea of discipline, and most of the time the rebels argued furiously among themselves, and even at times got to blows. They were all very excited and were in a boastful mood, and Tex watched them pityingly. They had his sympathy and he knew that what lay ahead of them wasn't good to contemplate.

They didn't see much of ex-Nazi General Sturmer that day. He kept as far away from them as possible, and proceeded without enthusiasm to try to get rebels to throw up proper breastworks, and then instruct them in the art of firing from cover. He was probably no more successful in his methods than the other legionnaires though all that day they could hear his loud, imperative voice shouting orders to a mob, which didn't want to understand them.

In the late afternoon the legionnaires found themselves without men to train. The novelty of being soldiers was wearing off with the increasing heat of the afternoon, and one by one those 'soldiers of freedom' began to drift away to where there was shade, where they could lie and doze and wait for the coolness of evening. The legionnaires walked across and stood grouped together to discuss the situation.

Joe was emphatic. 'I ain't gonna dig 'em out. I'm just as tired of playin' soldiers as these guys.' He was a weary and painfully angry man, Joe Ellighan.

Dimmy, good nature still beaming from his large round, simple face, nodded agreement. He wanted rest, too. So they all drifted back to the palace, where they found Nicky and Mahfra engaged in the feminine occupation of trying on Sheik Mahmoud's daughter's wardrobe. They all sat down together to discuss the situation yet again. It seemed they were forever discussing the situation, and never being able to do anything about it.

Then it was that Nicky realised that Tex wasn't joining in the conversation much, and suddenly a shrewd suspicion came into her quick mind. She moved across and sat against the big legionnaire. He smiled down on her. The rest was doing her a lot of good, and she looked her old bright, attractive self again.

'What are you thinking?' Nicky asked softly, her blue eyes looking up into that lean brown muscular face of the legionnaire from Texas.

Tex shrugged his shoulders and tried to be noncommittal. But Nicky shook her head.

She said, accusingly: 'You're planning

something, Tex. Now, come on, out with it, and let me know what you're up to!'

She spoke with a smile on her lips, and yet there was a little icy clutch to her heart, for she knew this big legionnaire and she knew he was capable of sacrificing himself in order to help his companions. He meant more to Nicky than all the world and she wasn't going to let him sacrifice himself for their sake if she could help it.

But Tex just looked with good humour from his lazy, grey eyes and drawled: 'Me? I'm not thinkin' of anythin', sweetheart. I'm just tired an' tryin' to get the ache out of my bones.'

She wasn't deceived, but though she tried to wheedle the truth out of him, he maintained that pose of tiredness, with even a degree of astonishment that she should think him 'up to something'.

In the end she gave it up, and lay beside him while the sun declined towards the coolness of evening. It was about an hour before sunset when, distantly, they heard the thin cry of the lookout man posted upon the tower where the flag flew over the fortress-palace. For a moment no one moved. In the dullness, which had descended on them with their afternoon's siesta, they did not comprehend the significance of that cry.

And then Tex lurched to his feet, upsetting Nicky as he did so, and ran to where the shutters were thrown back from the tall, open windows. He looked against the reddening sky, and saw the silhouette of that hooded Arab high up on the tower. He saw the arm outstretched and the finger pointing westward, and then the watcher's shrill cry was repeated and now it was taken up by Arabs resting in the shadows of the palace walls.

Tex turned at once and leapt to where his Lebel was propped against the wall. He shouted: 'Outside, you men! Mahmound is comin'!'

This wasn't their war. They had really no part in it, but they knew they had to fight, and fight hard and well if they were to save their lives — though there was a big question mark about the future even if they did help to defeat Sheik Mahmoud's army.

So now they raced down the broad, curving marble stairs, into the hall where Arabs were shuttling madly to and fro like ants in a disturbed ant heap.

Everyone was shouting, giving orders. No one was listening, and certainly no one was obeying any of the instructions. They had lost their heads because they were not soldiers and were not used to emergencies.

Tex realized this as he came bounding down the stairs. He must have looked a mighty, formidable figure in his faded blue tunic and his white fatigue trousers, the neck curtain of his hastily donned kepi flowing out as he ran. He was brandishing his Lebel rifle as if it were a toy in his hand.

In Arabic he shouted: 'Outside, everyone. Get your guns and go out to the trenches!'

Then he and the legionnaires drove the shouting, gesticulating mob out of that big hall and into the sunshine beyond. Once they were outside, a lot of Arabs did seem to recover their senses, perhaps recognising the gravity of their situation all in an instant. When the legionnaires ran to the outskirts of the town they followed and got down into the trenches where they had been placed earlier that afternoon.

The legionnaires and Sturmer and the more resolute members of the Brotherhood who had been brought by that rusting steamer to spearhead this revolt, managed to get some sort of order among their troops. At any rate they got them into the trenches, and saw that all had their rifles loaded and ready for use. Then the legionnaires ran from trench to trench, shouting encouragement and instructing their men not to fire until they were given orders to do so.

The thing was to let Mahmoud ride on towards the town until he was well within range of those rifles in the unsuspected trenches. If they held their fire until even the rebels, unused to guns, could hardly miss, then Mahmoud's army might be dealt a crippling blow.

Might! But Tex wasn't optimistic.

He ran across to where a mound reared at the back of a flat-topped native dwelling. He got onto the roof and looked westward. About a couple of miles away a dust cloud hung in the air, and the size of it indicated the movement of a large body of men.

Two miles. That meant that within minutes the cavalry would be upon them.

Tex jumped down and shouted the news to the legionnaires, each of whom had taken over a section of trench in an effort to maintain control over the nervous, chattering defenders.

Tex looked at those ragged men who had been overworked and undernourished labourers and peasants all their lives, and he saw the anxious rolling of eyes and knew they were near to panic even before Mahmoud attacked. His heart sank. It wasn't fair to expect these poor people to acquit themselves under such circumstances. These men weren't made for soldiering, and the Greek should have known it but had become lost in his own ego and confidence.

Tex got down with his men and ordered them to load and remove safety catches, where their old-fashioned weapons had any. Then they waited.

Not more than three or four minutes later the van of Mahmoud's army came riding out of the dust and began to manoeuvre within half a mile of the trenches that had been dug on the outskirts of the little mud town. Here the land was flat and devoid of vegetation save for an occasional tuft of coarse grass that survived in the sandy soil. They saw hundreds of horsemen, impressive desert warriors in their many-coloured robes, each with a rifle held above his head as they circled round and round some leader who was doubtless giving them last minute instructions.

Tex's blood tingled as he watched the manoeuvring of these superb horsemen. If he had any hopes before, they died now at sight of that impressive throng. The rebels couldn't stand up for long against the fierce and trained desert fighters.

He saw the Bedouins sort themselves out, so that they stretched in a long line, quite half a mile in extent, out there on the desert. They were trotting very slowly towards the trenches, and Tex prayed that his men would keep under cover and would certainly not betray themselves with a premature rifle shot.

Then, all at once, the line of horsemen leapt into top speed and Mahmoud's cavalry came in a wild charge.

Behind them another line of cavalry formed up as a second assault wave.

But Tex was only interested in defeating the first line of horsemen.

They came with rifles waving, with pennant-tipped lances erect like standards, and Mahmoud's men sent up a wild, blood-curdling war cry that must have chilled the hearts of those *fellahin* rebels in the trenches.

It happened exactly as Tex had prophesied.

The moment that charge began, some fool lost his head and fired wildly. That betrayed their position in the trenches; and then someone bolted for it, running in among the buildings towards the solid walls of the fortress. At once from every trench terrified rebels began to stream away from the charging cavalry. All in one moment the noisy, swaggering confidence in the peasants evaporated.

Suddenly the glamour of war deserted them, and they felt as always, weak, defenceless creatures. Sight of those madly-charging horsemen broke their nerve and sent them fleeing in terrified confusion.

Tex and his legionnaires tried to hold them back, but it was useless. Within seconds the trenches were mostly deserted. The men who remained were, on the whole, those men who had come into Dusa on that rusty old tramp steamer — they were the men of the Brotherhood who were dedicated to this fight for freedom because they had suffered more than most men.

The Brothers were resolute, and they shouted and swore at their craven-hearted allies, and when this failed to stop the desertion the Tormented Men merely sighted their rifles and prepared to die alone.

In a way, though, that sudden mass desertion deceived Mahmoud's charging cavalry. It gave the appearance of complete rout even before a shot was fired, and so the cavalry charged on with a reckless abandon that proved their own undoing.

For when they were about eighty yards

from the hidden trenches, a withering fire rose from that sparse line of grim defenders, and it was unexpected because it had seemed to Mahmoud's men that there was to be no defence of the town.

There were screams and groans of pain, and men fell off their charging horses. And many horses went down to add to the mad confusion. The dust rose and obscured the fallen, so that other horses ran onto them and more were brought down.

The defenders in their trenches fired until their rifles were hot in their hands. All the time Mahmoud's cavalry was trying to fight its way forward, to get into those trenches and come to grips with the few valiant defenders.

But they were beaten off, and the resistance grew so hot that they had to turn away and ride back to where the second wave waited to begin its charge. In the trenches they watched them go, and then they looked out upon the wounded who tried to crawl away and upon the feebly kicking horses that were alive and yet badly hurt.

Tex scrambled across to where Rube

was. His face was grim. He said: 'We won't stop the next assault when it comes!'

Rube nodded agreement. 'You're dead right, we won't!' he said emphatically.

Tex swung round to look at the nearby buildings.

He said: 'We'll have to do some street fightin', I reckon,' and Rube knew what he meant by that.

It meant retreating, and defending every building as they went back.

Rube said: 'That won't give us victory in the end. We'll fall back within the walls of the palace, and mebbe then we'll be able to hold 'em out for a few hours. But they'll dig us out or burn us out — or just shoot us out of existence. But we won't win in the end.'

He was stating the truth and not indulging in pessimism.

Tex nodded. He said: 'You're right at that, Rube. But keep fightin'. We'll get no quarter from Mahmoud, so while we've any bullets left in our belts, we must defend ourselves.' And then he ended, enigmatically: 'Mebbe something will turn up to help us.'

Rube looked quickly at the big Texan, not understanding. He saw that Tex's eyes were far away on the western horizon. But before he could question his comrade, Tex told him to pull his men out and take up positions in the buildings. They had too few to defend these long trench lines now, and he wanted to get them back into the shelter of the mud hovels before the second assault came upon them.

The defenders were brought out of their trenches, and ran quickly to where the outlying buildings of this sprawling little town began. When they saw them bolting for cover, Mahmoud's forces set up a yell of hate and triumph. They weren't properly formed up, but before an order could be given, the whole line began to ride forward. The canter became a gallop, and then the gallop became a mad charge with rifles blazing off recklessly at the fleeing Arabs and their few Foreign Legion companions.

Most of the defenders reached the safety of the buildings without suffering from the wild salvo of shots, however.

Then, from every possible vantage point behind cover, the Brotherhood and the legionnaires turned at bay and began to pump lead into the attackers.

The Arab cavalry tried to ride into the many alleyways that opened onto this desert, but they were driven back by a fire that was concentrated because the line had been shortened, and for several minutes there was a crazy confusion of horsemen manoeuvring out of each other's way and at the same time trying to shoot down the defenders from their saddles.

The defence had an advantage for the moment. Then a reckless young Arab came riding in, standing on his saddle. He flung himself on top of a building, and crawled across the roof and dropped down into the roadway beyond. His example was followed by many of his comrades, so that all in one moment the defences were breached, and Arabs were infiltrating and attacking from the defenders' rear.

This meant a retreat, and it was quick, with every man running madly deeper into the town. Now the triumphant Arab horsemen came pouring in off the desert, their shouts ringing, and their lances waving because they thought that victory was theirs all in that moment.

The sun's rays, almost horizontal because darkness was close upon them, illuminated that savage battle scene. The defenders rallied at every possible point and hit back at a more powerful, vindictive enemy. They didn't stop the rush, but at least they held them back for minutes at a time.

Darkness had fallen, when word spread among the defenders to abandon the town. They would not be able to hold it against the enemy now that light had gone.

The defenders began to run towards the nearest gates of the fortress-palace, and many were ridden down by vengeful, shouting horsemen, but most managed to get through the gateways. Then the mighty bars were dropped into position and Mahmoud's fortress was being used against his army.

For hours in the moonlight Mahmoud's horsemen rode around the fortress, trying to find a place by which to enter. All the time, defenders sniped at them from the wall-tops and from the towers, and they inflicted a lot of damage upon Mahmoud's hot-headed young warriors.

About midnight, Mahmoud called off the attack. They saw fires raging through the town where Mahmoud's men had taken revenge upon people they suspected of complicity in the revolt, and soon a whole quarter of the town was in flames. Mahmoud had captured Dusa, even if his own palace was still held by the rebels.

Wearily the legionnaires came together, as they always did when they had opportunity. Suleiman was with them and Nicky came down to the courtyard and brought them food and drink, and they were grateful for both.

Dimmy was the last to join them. He came over and drank from the water jar, and then wiped his perspiring face. He said: 'Things don't look so good.'

Rube shook his head. 'Things don't look so good,' he agreed. 'It's only a question of time before Mahmoud's men scale a wall and get in among us.'

They stood there in the moonlight, and

there was gloom upon them. It wasn't a pleasant feeling to know that a savage and brutal enemy had completely encircled them now, so that there was no way of escape out of the palace.

Nicky drifted away among the tired Arab defenders who were lying down wherever they could find space in that crowded courtyard. Rube watched her walking among the Arabs, looking very white in the moonlight.

After a time his head lifted, for he began to notice something about the way in which Nicky walked. She seemed to be hurrying, and there seemed no need for her to be moving quickly, as she was. She was going from group to group, and she seemed to be . . . looking for someone.

She disappeared from sight, and Rube forgot about it for a few moments, and then suddenly he saw Nicky coming into view from another direction. He saw that she was almost running. He straightened himself, and said to his companions, quickly: 'Nicky's in trouble. I wonder what it is this time?'

They turned at once, for Nicky was

loved by every one of those legionnaires.

They saw her run towards them, her face pale in the moonlight. Before she reached them they all guessed what it was.

As she ran up they heard her call: 'Where's Tex?'

They looked at each other. They had missed Tex, but had felt vaguely that he would be somewhere around and would turn up any minute. But now that Nicky had spoken they began to feel suddenly alarmed.

Rube said: 'I don't know where he is. Has anyone seen him?' Nicky shook her head and they could see the agony in her eyes. 'I looked all over the courtyard, but he's not here. I'm sure he'd be somewhere out here with the men — if he were inside the fortress.'

That jarred on them, the implication of her sentence.

Joe yapped, quickly: 'I ain't seen him since we were out at them trenches.' He looked round at the others questioningly.

Rube said, slowly: 'That's where I saw him last.'

And that's where Dimmy had seen him last, too.

An icy breath swept over them then. They felt sure in that moment that disaster had come to their big-hearted comrade. He wasn't within the fortress — of that they felt sure by now. And the alternative was that he was lying outside, hurt or dead.

Joe said: 'I'm goin' out to find him.'

But when they all went across to a gate the Brothers would not let them out. If Tex was on the other side of the wall, he could not look to them for aid.

They turned away, defeated. And all of them felt sure that they had seen the last of big Tex.

8

'Ride With the Spahis!'

Tex didn't go after the legionnaires and the other defenders when they retreated in among the buildings. He'd had it all mapped out in his mind for the past hour what he was going to do.

The one thing he knew he wasn't going to do was to allow himself to be penned in by Mahmoud's forces and butchered at their convenience. He was a fighter, but a man with brains and ingenuity, and he had seen a way of saving Dusa from Mahmoud's men and he wasn't forgetting the idea.

Obstinately he was determined to bring the French in on this war, and use them to turn the tables on Mahmoud's much stronger forces. He could think of no other way of saving his companions' lives, and the lives of these poor devils who had revolted against a tyrannical hierarchy.

He dropped back into his trench, having made a pretence of starting towards the buildings with the others, and crouched down in the manner of a man hurt or killed. As he lay there he heard the thunder of approaching hooves, and the wild shouts of the blood-lusting desert warriors. Then the noise grew to an intensity of sound, and he felt forms leaping across that trench, as horseman after horseman took it in his stride. Dirt and stones showered down upon him, but he lay there unmoving.

For he knew that if he moved he would be shot down in an instant.

Then the noise receded as the cavalry charge swept on towards the outlying buildings of Dusa. When it seemed that no others were racing up Tex cautiously lifted himself out of the muck and peered over the edge of the breastwork.

There was so much dust and powder-smoke blowing about this part of the desert that everything appeared dim and distorted as in a fog. Even the setting sun was temporarily eclipsed.

He heard the fierce fighting a quarter

of a mile back of him, where the alleys ran out onto the scrub desert, and he heard the incessant rattle of guns and sometimes even the clash of steel upon steel.

Mahmoud's men were triumphant, and their war cries came floating clearly to his ears. But he couldn't see them — couldn't see the battle that was raging for the town — because of that cloud of dust that had been kicked up.

He climbed out of the trench, holding his Lebel grimly, and crouching ready for instant action if an enemy loomed up. Then he saw a riderless horse trotting away from the noise of battle. He began to run, then, his long legs taking him in great bounds across the hard-baked desert. The horse saw him coming, and being a horse it started to run away.

Tex put his head down and went flat out to get it before it eluded him. He caught it by the mane, and in one lithe, rolling motion swung at top speed into the saddle. He did it effortlessly, like the born horseman he was, and the horse seemed amazed that it had been caught and mounted so easily.

Then they ran out of the dust cloud as a hot, westerly wind came blowing up from the desert to disperse it . . .

Tex realised the danger instantly.

All across the desert were parties of Arab stragglers, loping along to catch up with the main attacking force. He saw flowing robes and streaming manes, as eager desert warriors came riding to be in at the death. And far behind on the horizon he could see the baggage train of Mahmoud's forces, slower than the cavalry, but well-guarded and with plenty of mounted men riding around it.

There were three Arabs within a hundred yards of him, and when they saw that hated blue uniform they came in screaming their war cry — '*Allah-o-Akba!*'

Tex swerved his horse but there was insufficient room for manoeuvring, and the three Arabs cut across to intercept him. There was nothing else for it but to fight his way through. The Arabs had fired their guns, which were now obviously empty, and they were charging in to finish him off with their flashing scimitars.

Big Tex deliberately swerved his horse again and this time he sent it crashing into the trio. His Lebel swung over his head, and he had long arms and out-reached those swordsmen. The heavy butt crashed onto the neck of a bearded, fanatically-eyed Bedouin, and Tex saw the man roll out of his saddle.

Then Tex's horse ran into the other two beasts and immediately went down on its knees and threw Tex. Tex went head over heels in the desert, and even as he was falling a clamouring thought was in his mind — 'I've got to get a hoss! I'm dead meat if I'm caught here on the desert un-mounted.'

He came onto his feet in one lithe movement, and he was still gripping his precious rifle. He saw that his horse had hurt itself in that charge and was limping away, and so he jumped towards the nearest beast, and came in with his Lebel swinging savagely again. The Arab on the horse tried to parry the blow, but Tex beat down his defences, and knocked him half-unconscious where he sat trying to evade the powerful blow.

Tex grabbed the sandalled foot and heaved the Arab out of his polished, ornamented saddle.

The other Arab was coming in, his expression vicious. He must have been loading his rifle, for he raised it, and there was murder in his eyes.

Tex threw himself sideways and in that same movement his hand dived in a practised draw and out came the revolver from his belt. The Arab never pulled the trigger. He just fell from his saddle and rolled over in the dust and was still for a few minutes and then painfully got to his feet and walked away holding a shattered shoulder.

He didn't know that he owed his life to a generous enemy. He didn't know that big Tex could have killed him just as easily as he had winged him.

But by this time Tex was hundreds of yards away. He had dived for one of the horses and caught it, and was in the saddle and was going hell-for-leather across the scrub desert.

He wasn't out of the wood yet. It isn't easy to break through the lines of an enemy, especially an enemy as mobile as Arabs. He saw a body of horsemen detach themselves from the distant baggage train, and he settled down in the saddle to outride them, if it were possible.

But after a while he realised that the horse he was riding had been hard-ridden during that day and it began to labour very early on in the race. The horsemen from the baggage train had probably been moving at walking pace most of the day and so their horses were much the fresher.

Tex looked at the sun, which was partly obscured by the ragged range of western hills, and tried to calculate how long he had to keep going before darkness came to hide his movements.

But long before darkness was upon him, those madly galloping Bedouins were in a position before him. He swerved northwards now, though it was out of his way, and this brought him riding in a parallel position to his attackers.

He saw them crowding in, their robes almost straight in the wind created by their swift passage. He saw the open slavering jaws of their mettlesome steeds. And he saw rifles leaping into the hands of that strong party of Arab horsemen, and knew it was time he acted.

He pulled an old Indian trick on them, one that every cowboy on the Western ranges knew. He slid down the side of his mount, his left foot crooked over his saddle bow, one arm holding his Lebel around the neck of his galloping horse. And he fired his revolver from under the head of the terrified animal.

The manoeuvre foxed his pursuers for a moment. Just for a few seconds they hadn't the sense to shoot at the horse and bring both it and rider down. So it was that Tex emptied his revolver into the ranks of those horsemen, and he fired at man or beast and created havoc.

He saw a horse go head over heels, throwing its rider yards ahead into the scrub. He saw the other horsemen run on to it and pile up, and it always happened like that. These Arab horsemen were too impetuous. He fired at the few who were pulling round, and with it all he found himself suddenly streaking into the lead.

But that lead wasn't much use to him. His horse was blown and couldn't keep up this pace for more than a few seconds longer.

So deliberately, one eye on that western sky, Tex pulled it down to a slow walk, and then turned in his saddle and waited for his pursuers to come up. There were about nine of them left in the race now, with more trying to catch their mounts and come on afterwards. But for the moment these nine were important.

Tex sat round comfortably in his saddle, and sighted his Lebel on the leading Arab and shot him clean out of the saddle. He put another round into the breech, sighted again, and another Arab was thrown off his horse. Tex didn't like doing it. He had a conscience where killing was concerned, but he was also a man who wanted to live, and this was a case of kill or be killed.

His third shot missed. They were pulling out now, and were fanning out to surround him. They opened up with their guns, too, but their weapons weren't a match for the French-made rifle, and though their bullets spanged closely they did no damage.

Tex looked at the sun, which still showed above the western horizon, and then he sighted and fired and there were only six Arabs left to surround him. He walked his horse steadily northwards, and the Arabs completely encircled him. Now there were Arabs in front and on all sides and behind him.

He saw a couple of them come swerving in, determined to ride him down from his left flank. He fired the last two rounds in his rifle, and each time he fired at the bigger target — the horse — and he brought them both down and their Arab riders with them.

But the other four Arabs were closing in, too, and their bullets were hitting now. He felt his horse shudder and knew that it had been hit. After a few minutes it stopped walking and began to tremble, and he got off, knowing that it had had its death blow. He walked away from it. The sun had set now, but those four riders were circling within eighty yards of him, and their guns were being reloaded.

He had time to slip two rounds into his magazine, and he fired quickly at one who was already sighting. He must have hit the man, and disturbed his aim, but the gun went off and the bullet narrowly missed Tex all the same. Then, beginning to run now, dodging so as to present an elusive target, Tex fired his second round.

That missed altogether. He kept running, and for a few vital minutes the Arabs got together in a group to decide on tactics.

Some other Arabs came riding up now, and in the fading light they must have decided that the only thing was to make one wild charge upon this death-dealing, blue-tunicked infidel. Tex saw them break into a gallop and he ran to where a rocky outcrop reared man-high in the desert.

He got down against it and reloaded and began to fire. But the light was fading so rapidly and these riders were coming in at a swirling gallop so he didn't seem to hit at all. Only when they were at point-blank range did he see one of the Arabs fall back off his horse.

He had been waiting for that. The

riderless horse came crashing up along with the other riders. Big Tex deliberately lunged forward, towards the attack, and with that same lightning move of the practised cowpuncher, he hurled himself into the saddle of the riderless horse as it galloped madly past him. He didn't even use his hands in making that leap, for he was firing with his Lebel even as he jumped for the saddle.

It startled the Arabs. These sort of tactics were too unexpected for them to be able to assimilate. They found themselves riding in a bunch around the big American legionnaire. For a few seconds they all seemed to ride together, and Tex had time to think how incongruous the situation was.

He was within a couple of yards of one Arab, with the others no more than fifteen or twenty yards away on either side of him. In the near-darkness he saw swarthy faces and black beards and surprised, flashing eyes. It seemed that not one of those Arabs had a round left in his rifle, otherwise Tex couldn't have escaped at that moment.

They came at him with their guns wielded as clubs and with their sharp, flashing scimitars wielded to deal him a deathblow.

Tex wasn't going to wait for any deathblow. His guns were empty, and he had no time to reload, but he kept his horse racing across the desert, swerving it with pressure of his knees so that always he was going away from the main body of attackers. They came at him, time after time, and he parried their thrusts with his swinging Lebel. And when he had opportunity he lashed out viciously and had the satisfaction of seeing his blows take effect.

One turbaned Arab was knocked clean out of his saddle, and two others went pulling out of the fight when he hit them with the brass-bound butt of his gun.

And all the time darkness was falling, and Tex knew that he was winning this race.

There came a time, in fact, when they could not see each other at more than twenty or thirty yards' range, and then Tex stopped fighting and lay low across the neck of his horse, and he seemed to lift it at every stride and take it at headlong pace out of range of his pursuers and out of vision, too. It was a pace that couldn't last, but when he felt he was out of sight, he swerved violently and ran a hundred yards at right angles to his original course. Then he halted his sweating beast and sat there silently and listened to the pursuit go racing by.

He stood there for five or ten minutes, resting his horse, and after that he never once heard from his pursuers. He had given them the slip.

He began to walk his horse, allowing it to recover from its recent ordeal. The stars were out and soon there would be a moon to help him, but for the moment he went cautiously in a northerly direction because he could not wait and waste time when he knew that his comrades in Dusa might now be fighting for their lives.

It was just before dawn when a sentry on the edge of Oasis Khasr-el-Juba sent out a challenging cry. *'Halte! Qui va la?'*

Tex, riding in upon his jaded horse, called: 'I am one of you, *mon petit.'*

The sentry crouched behind his rifle, watching through the grey mist of early morning as the desert-dusty legionnaire came slowly towards him. Then he recognised the uniform and relaxed.

Tex swung down and walked the remaining distance, leading his horse. He took it to water, and left it there, while he went along the tent lines that were grouped under the gracious palm trees that flourished in this desert oasis. In the growing light he began to see the situation in the camp, and he walked across to where the officers' tents were erected by a standard that during daylight hours would fly the tricoleur.

He saw an orderly and called that he wanted to see the officer in charge.

'Le Generale Aristide?'

Tex could have groaned when he heard the name. General Jean Aristide was the biggest handicap that France had in her colonial plans in North Africa.

He was a small, fussy man, who thought a lot about detail, but never seemed to comprehend the major features of strategy. He would argue long about the design on a regimental badge, and ignore the fact that that regiment was using pre-1914 rifles. This didn't augur well for snap decisions, demanding a swift march on the part of the French soldiers to nearby Hejib.

Tex said, all the same: 'I want to see him immediately. It's urgent.'

The orderly, a slatternly fellow, as all orderlies are, a thin Moroccan cigarette drooping from his down-turned mouth, looked cynically at the big, untidy legionnaire. '*Mon ami,* you must surely be bitten by *le cafard* to want to meet *le generale* in your condition.'

His hand waved towards the untidiness and the dirt that was familiar on Tex's uniform these days. 'He will surely put you in *les cellules* if you do not first shave and clean your buttons and perfect your toilet,' the man said, and he meant well in his advice.

Tex said, tiredly: 'There is no time for that. I must see *le generale* now.'

But the orderly hadn't the faintest intention of waking the general. Things happened to orderlies who disturbed generals' sleep. In the end he compromised by awakening the adjutant, a lean-faced pessimistic-looking captain who wanted to know at once what regiment Tex belonged to.

Tex had his story all ready, and it satisfied the captain. Since the Arab revolt there were many men wandering alone in the desert since the desert battles of the past few weeks.

Impatiently Tex gave his replies, and then he came to the important part of his presence before the officer. He said: 'Sheik Mahmoud has been turned out of his kingdom in the Hejib. The people of Hejib have got tired of this warmonger, and have seized Dusa and his palace in his absence. Now he is trying to recapture it by force, and it presents France with a great opportunity of liquidating such a vicious enemy.'

The light was increasing in intensity now, as the sun came up. Birds were chattering in the trees above the tent in which the tall legionnaire stood and faced a captain dishevelled from his bed. The captain said nothing but looked at Tex with brown, lugubrious eyes and listened.

'France could send her troops in now

and there would be no fear of international situations,' Tex urged. 'The new government of Hejib would welcome the intervention of France's forces if it removed Sheik Mahmoud and his men. We could, by forced marches, come upon Mahmoud from his rear while he is engaged in attacking the town.'

Tex felt irritated by the captain's silence. He had expected enthusiasm and a great deal of running about and shouting of orders. But this pessimistic-looking man didn't reveal any sign of emotion.

When finally he did speak, his question was: 'Why are you so anxious to get back to Dusa?' He was shrewder than he looked, that brown-eyed, doleful-faced captain.

Tex told him — 'The Arabs have three of my compatriots prisoner, as well as an American girl. I want to save their lives, and they will die if they fall into Mahmoud's hands.'

He didn't say that they were likely to die regardless of whose hands they were in after this battle for Dusa. That would have introduced unnecessary complications into the conversation.

It seemed to satisfy the captain, who might have thought the whole plan a trick on the part of some renegade legionnaire. He hastily finished his toilet and then went across to speak with other officers before the general deigned to rise from his bed. Tex went in search of food and drink, and he took the precaution of cleaning himself up in case he was summoned before the general.

He told some of his companions of the situation — they were strangers to him, though of the Foreign Legion, being of another regiment.

As they sat around in the warming rays of the new-risen sun and ate their breakfasts, there was discussion about the situation. They were men of many nationalities and with many reasons for being in the Foreign Legion. But few had joined the Legion because of a love for fighting.

Now the talk was against going into Hejib to fight another battle with Mahmoud. They had no illusions about war, and to them it was an uncomfortable experience fraught with many dangers. For their part, they could stay in this oasis as long as they liked, and if they never saw another Arab enemy that suited them.

Tex could understand their point of view, but he was impatient with it, because the lives of good comrades were at stake, and also the life of the lovely blonde American newspaperwoman whom he had grown to love.

He had also a sympathy with the rebels in the Hejib — the sympathy that is always given to the underdog. Those people had suffered under the tyrant Mahmoud and he would have been better pleased to have seen them triumphant.

When he found the conversation was against another battle with Mahmoud, Tex dropped the subject. He was determined to bring the French onto the enemy, and he waited with fuming impatience for some decision of the officers' conference.

After a time he was summoned to the general's tent There were many officers there, and some he recognised though they would not know him, a mere legionnaire. He saw General Aristide, a dried-up, quick-moving little man in a pillbox of a hat decorated with too much gold braid. He was finding fault with the positioning of the tent lines when Tex arrived. They were not in parallel rows, he was complaining, and it was unmilitary to see such disorderliness.

There was an old colonel there, who led the Spahis, the French native cavalry troops who had such a high reputation in desert campaigns. He was abrupt to the general in a manner that was unusual.

He said: '*Mon generale*, it is not possible to set tents out in orderly lines when there are trees intervening and great roots which would make for uncomfortable lying for some of the men.'

General Aristide was indignant immediately. What did he care about the comfort of a few men? They were soldiers and should learn to sleep just as comfortably on tree roots as on beds. Did *he* ever complain?

Nobody answered that question, though a comfortable bed in the corner was a silent witness to a possible line of thought in those officers' minds.

The general was saying that if necessary a few trees should be chopped down, and at that there was a gasp of horror from some of the officers. For trees were more precious than human lives in these parts. But General Aristide wanted his pretty pattern of tent lines and he was determined to get them.

Tex heard all this standing on the fringe of the group of officers, respectfully listening to that fussy little officer in the general's hat. His thoughts were grim. Aristide was the kind of man who fiddled while Rome burned — who bothered about tent lines when military strategy on a high plane should have been the subject of discussion.

The colonel of the Spahis was looking at Tex, and Tex found his gaze attracted to the man. This colonel was of different breed to the little general. He was a man of medium height, and grey above the temples and in his rather heavy, ragged moustache. Around his eyes were wrinkles, as if he had lived his life mostly where the sun shone brightly, but the eyes that looked at Tex weren't faded with age, but were sharp and betokened the mind of a clear-thinking man.

Now this colonel broke in on the important discourse about tent lines, saying: '*Mon generale,* there is a matter of greater urgency than tent lines, I beg leave to suggest. Here we have a legionnaire who brings momentous news — that if we act quickly we can trap the rebel Arab forces between two fires and eliminate a man who has always been a trouble to France.'

The general waved his hand impatiently. 'All this can be discussed later,' he said irritably. 'We will not move from this oasis until we have satisfactorily settled this matter of the tent lines.'

The officers looked at each other. The general was more asinine than usual. He was simply not prepared to discuss this possibility of routing Mahmoud, and became imperative in his speech when the colonel again raised the subject.

So Tex was ordered away, because if the general didn't want to hear his story, then no one else apparently would be able to listen to it. No one could do anything about it in any event without the general's approval.

He was walking away, rage consuming him that France should have her interests resting in the hands of incompetents like General Aristide, when a sharp order brought him to a standstill, stiffly to attention.

The colonel of Spahis was striding after him.

The colonel stood before him, returning his salute, his grim, grey eyes looking at the tall Texan under bushy, greying eyebrows. He said: 'You are disappointed, *mon petit?*'

Stiffly, Tex replied: 'I am disappointed, *mon colonel*. The lives of my friends are in danger, and they mean more to me than anything. I am disappointed, too, because here is an opportunity for France to put an end to this desert war which Sheik Mahmoud continually wages.'

The colonel nodded grimly. 'It is as you say, but the general in his wisdom has seen fit to set other things in importance above an expedition against Mahmoud. You will realise, of course, that until General Aristide gives his authority, it is impossible to take troops into action against the Bedouins?'

Tex's heart was sinking, but he answered: 'That is to be understood, *mon colonel.*'

The colonel was looking towards the Spahi lines, where North African troops were grooming and preparing their horses for the day. The colonel seemed to be talking to himself now, rather than to that big legionnaire. 'It is not possible for *le generale* to find fault with the Spahi lines.' That was true, because the Spahis did not sleep under tents. Therefore there could be no question of their tents being out of line with others.

The colonel's grey eyes swung back to Tex's. He said: 'My men would be better riding out on manoeuvres today. I will take them for a brief canter into the desert.'

Tex's eyes were suddenly intent upon the colonel.

The colonel said: 'In view of *le generale*'s reluctance to meet Mahmoud until the tent lines are completed, it would be unwise for my Spahis to practise their manoeuvres where they might run into combat with Mahmoud's men.'

Tex licked his lips, not daring to believe what was leaping into his mind. He said, quickly: 'It would not be a good thing, as you have said, *mon colonel.*'

The colonel slapped his polished leggings with a riding switch, and now his eyes had removed themselves again from Tex's intent face. He said: 'Perhaps, *mon legionnaire*, it would be better if you rode out with my Spahis, in order to keep me away from where you last saw the enemy forces.'

Tex said: 'Perhaps that would be in accordance with *le generale's* desires.'

Then the eyes of the colonel and the legionnaire met, and there was understanding between them.

The colonel strode off, shouting to his officers, and within minutes those Spahis were saddling up their horses, and leading them out from the shade of the palm trees, into the hot, yellow desert that lay to the south of it. And with them rode one blue-tunicked infantryman of France's Foreign Legion.

Tex knew what was expected of him. This resolute colonel wanted to take his Spahis against Mahmoud's forces, and Tex intended to help him.

9

The Palace

Tex was given a spare horse to ride, and was ordered to keep up with the colonel, who led out the Spahis. They had two hundred men in all, a strong, resolute fighting force, but hardly a big enough company with which to attack Mahmoud's army.

But these Spahis were better armed than the Bedouins, and the colonel, no doubt, was banking on the fact that the rebels inside Dusa would be able to take care of some part of Mahmoud's army. Therefore two hundred men might, by a sudden pounce, rout a far bigger army.

Tex wasn't optimistic, but he didn't allow pessimism to affect his thoughts. All he cared about was that he was taking some assistance into the Hejib that might save the lives of his friends — and Nicky.

All day they rode in a cloud of dust that

must have betrayed them for miles around if anyone had been watching for them. But they reckoned that within Dusa everyone would be concerned with the attack on the fortress and wouldn't have eyes for an approaching column coming out of the northern desert.

They rested their horses for three hours during the heat of the day, and though Tex was impatient with the long halt, he recognised the wisdom of it. It would have been folly to have ridden into battle with Mahmoud's Arabs upon horses which were foundering from fatigue.

About four in the afternoon they resumed their steady ride across the desert. When they were a few miles from Dusa, and inside Hejib territory now, they saw a cloud of black smoke ahead of them. Tex's heart stood still. It seemed to him that the whole town must be on fire. When they came nearer, Tex realised that more than the town was on fire.

The fortress-palace was ablaze from end to end, and to Tex and the Spahis it didn't seem possible that anyone could remain alive within it.

The big, brown-faced legionnaire looked on that sight while cold horror gripped his heart. It seemed to him that they had arrived too late.

They went on towards the town, quickening their pace now, and the wind was blowing in from the sea so that they ran into a dense smoke pall that made them choke and caused their eyes to stream, and hid them from view. It wasn't a comfortable way of approaching the town, but it had the advantage that at least their presence would be undetected.

They could hear gunfire, and the low roar of distant shouting voices suggested that a battle still raged around the harbour. The sky was red from the blazing buildings, and the smoke seemed to get thicker with the passing minutes.

Mahmoud and his men were exacting a terrible revenge upon the townspeople who had tried to overthrow him in his absence.

The Spahis were halted under cover of the first of the buildings of this Mediterranean seaport. They hugged the shelter, while the colonel dispatched a party of five Spahis under a lieutenant to reconnoitre the situation.

Tex waited his chance, and then gradually pulled his horse deeper into the swirling smoke until he was out of sight of the Spahis. He had no intention of remaining with French forces, and the sooner he got away from them the better. He sent his horse trotting down a narrow, deserted alley.

After a time he found himself against the high wall of the palace. This part of the town was completely devoid of human life . . . though there were bodies enough in plenty all around a broken gateway that gave access into the palace courtyard.

Holding his Lebel at the alert, Tex rode up to that shattered gateway. From this height he could look down over the harbour area now, and he realised that a battle was still raging where a rocky promontory formed part of the harbour itself. It was difficult to see what was happening, because every few moments the smoke from the blazing lower part of the town swept across the view and hid it from sight.

Tex went through the gate. He saw the mighty building, that had been one of the wonders of this northern coast of Africa, ablaze from end to end, and he knew as he looked at it that this was an act of the rebels themselves and not of Sheik Mahmoud. Mahmoud would not have destroyed his own palace.

Part of a roof crashed, and a cascade of sparks flew into the air and dropped among the palm trees that graced the inner courtyard. Tex's horse began to prance, terrified by the roaring, leaping flames and the sound of blazing floors falling through.

But Tex quieted the beast and sent it forward among the huddled corpses that lay within the high walls. He was looking — and dreading to see what he might find.

He went right across the big courtyard, and there was not a familiar blue uniform in all that array of tattered peasant *galabiers* and white Bedouin burnouses. He was filled with relief.

And then he came round the side of the palace where a broad walk led to pleasant rose gardens to the west of the palace. He reined abruptly.

Ahead of him, sprawled with a lance through his back, was a man who wore a blue tunic like his own.

Tex's eyes lifted in horror. He saw another blue tunicked figure, and another . . .

He came sliding off his horse, and went rushing forward, and yet he knew that the only legionnaires who had been in that palace were his comrades. They were all dead . . .

10

'Kill the Infidels!'

All that night the crowded garrison of the fortress-palace watched the carnage in the town of Dusa.

Mahmoud's men were riding through the town, searching out victims and slaughtering them and then setting fire to their miserable homes. This was their moment of revenge. This would teach these dogs of *fellahin* to rise against their masters!

With them rode Sheik Mahmoud himself, magnificent in his silken robes and with the gold threads on his *agal* that told of his patrician blood.

It was Mahmoud who directed the slaughter and encouraged the destruction of the town. His thin, bitter face filled with savage triumph as he saw the punishment that was meted out to the rebel townspeople. They would never forget this lesson, he vowed. And then he thought: 'Not many will live to remember it.'

But he was in a mood for insane destruction, and the whole night long he sent his troops searching and pillaging and burning. And his savage mercenaries obeyed him to the last letter and there were terrible deeds performed that night in the narrow alleys of that little Arab town.

All this they saw from the top floors of the palace. They saw the spreading red glow as half the town was fired as a lesson to the other half. And they coughed and spluttered as dense smoke came rolling over them.

Bedouin snipers had got into position outside the walls, so that it wasn't safe to stand revealed against the windows. Defenders replied to the fire but it never grew very brisk during the night and towards dawn in fact the firing ceased altogether.

Rube and the others ate what food they could find, in a room with the girls. They didn't feel particularly exhilarated. Their situation was critical and to add to it was the thought that their gallant leader had already fallen to the Arabs.

Nicky was suffering. She didn't let her sufferings affect her companions, but it seemed as if her heart was bleeding with grief because big Tex had failed to return.

They got some sleep during the night, but were called early, before dawn, by the Greek. There was a big meeting in the courtyard, and the Greek and the most determined of the Brothers who had been smuggled ashore to start this revolt addressed the crowd.

The legionnaires didn't understand Arabic very well and it was with difficulty that they realised what the situation was. It turned out that there were men among the rebels who were wanting to throw themselves on Mahmoud's mercy and not continue a resistance to the bitter end as the Greek was advocating.

Now the Greek — that handsome Arab who showed the foreign blood of his thousand-year-old ancestors — spoke to them tersely and contemptuously. The man who thought there was mercy in Mahmoud was a fool, was his contention.

No, they must fight to the last man, because tyrants should always be opposed and there should never be a compromise with them. If they were resolute now they might even defeat this army of Mahmoud and save their lives in victory.

He was inspiring in his address, but by now no one was deceived. They knew that Mahmoud's army was more than a match for these untrained rebels.

So it was that this group of dissidents gathered together and looked angrily at the Brothers who had brought them into this trouble. For as is the way with men, now they did not accept their share in the responsibility for events but rather sought to find scapegoats to fasten the whole blame upon them.

The Greek knew it and kept his brethren about him as he went about the preparations for the defence of the palace.

He posted men all along the walls and in the tower and even on the roof of the palace, and told them that soon an attack would develop and they had to fight for their lives and show no mercy.

The legionnaires took up positions in

the tower where their good rifles were of best advantage to the garrison.

Then they waited while dawn broke and the sun came up and turned a cool night into an inferno of a day. Down around the harbour the fire was spreading because there was no one there to control it, and the choking fumes added to the unpleasantness of the hot, dry morning.

Mahmoud attacked two hours after dawn, when his men had rested awhile. This time they came in afoot, firing from behind the shelter of the houses outside the palace walls. Because they were superior in numbers they did a lot of damage and the rebels lost heart and refused to man those suicidal positions under the enemy's fire.

The Greek went and tried to drive them back, but the *fellahin* were in a panic and feared the Greek less than they did the bullets from outside. So in the end the Greek and the brave Brotherhood manned the most dangerous points of the fortress wall. There were many who died, in the next few hours, of the force that had been recruited in every capital of

Arabia and had been brought into Hejib by a trick that was piracy.

About noon the battle rose in intensity. In the town the legionnaires realised the significance of it.

Mahmoud was putting up a tremendous barrage in order to keep down the heads of the defenders, and so permit a body of men armed with a battering ram to approach one of the gates.

Suddenly, up there in the tower, they heard a mighty crash as a massive beam, carried by fifty flowing-robed Bedouins, smashed into the big gates at the south entrance to the courtyard. Rube looked down quickly and saw that the gates had yielded even to that first blow, and at once he pulled Nicky to her feet, and shouted: 'Come on, let's get out of here. They'll be inside the courtyard within minutes!'

When they got down into the courtyard they realised that the gates were still holding, but there was savage fighting among the garrison itself. The men who wanted to compromise and talk and surrender to Mahmoud thought now that if they seized the Greek and members of the Brotherhood of Tormented Men the act might find clemency with the tyrant ruler of Hejib.

It was a treacherous thing to do, and it at once created the most bitter and savage hand-to-hand fighting.

Rube watched it for a second or two, and then said:

'We must get out of here. The fort can't hold out much longer.'

At that moment the gate reeled under another mighty blow from the battering ram, and then the Greek and his brethren, and their supporters among the rebels, came pouring back towards this corner where the rose garden was.

The Greek had seen that the game was up — that they could not fight an enemy outside while they were engaged with the enemy within the courtyard. It was not as if all the townspeople had suddenly had a change of heart; a good many were desperate enough to keep faith with the Brotherhood which had tried, after all, to improve their lot in life.

But a substantial number of Dusa

Arabs had become turncoats, and for the moment they were more dangerous than the enemy who was now frantically tearing at that weakening gate.

Suleiman came into view unexpectedly. They saw he was dragging Mahfra with him, and Mahfra was terrified out of her wits. She was not used to war, and especially to the terrifying din that accompanied Arab warfare.

Rube looked at her in her silken houri's costume, and he was aghast. He muttered: 'My God, if they catch you in those clothes . . . '

He knew that the Sheik's daughter would exact a terrible vengeance upon this peasant girl who had been placed in the position Souriya had formerly occupied.

Rube looked round him desperately. At that moment he heard the roar of flame close at hand, and he shouted: 'The palace is on fire!'

Suleiman was still holding onto Mahfra, and he shouted above the noise of the fighting men: 'The Greek ordered it. He won't let Mahmoud inherit much if he does win this battle!'

But Mahmoud was undoubtedly winning. The gate came partly open, and then it stuck and required several more blows with that ponderous battering ram.

When they looked round they realised that Rube was missing. Before they could become alarmed, however, he had returned, and in his arms were some Bedouin robes. He said, tersely: 'Don't argue! Get into these clothes. Now's the time when anybody who doesn't like the Foreign Legion will take a poke at us!'

He whipped off his tunic and hurled it onto a sprawling body under a rose arbour, and got into a burnouse and pulled the mouth-cloth across his face as if to keep out the bitter smoke clouds.

Dimmy and Joe were quick to get out of their tunics and into their robes, and then they helped the two girls to put on the all-enveloping cloaks.

Nicky asked: 'What now?'

The problem was solved for them. The gates smashed utterly, and a frenzied horde of Bedouins came piling into the courtyard. The Greek pulled his men back then, fighting all the way. He still had the better part of three hundred men loyal to him and they seemed determined to fight to the death. They came round the corner, so that in the confusion the disguised legionnaires and the girls were in danger of becoming separated. The movement of the crowd carried them right round the blazing palace, towards a rear gate.

They didn't realise it but there was a plan even in this apparent confusion. That plan was to break out of this fortress-palace, which was no longer defendable. The Greek had a rearguard holding back the exultant Bedouins, while some of the brethren raced to a gate and opened it in the face of Bedouins posted beyond.

They had to fight their way through a gathering crowd of Bedouins who came rushing up when they saw the attempt to leave the palace by this rear exit. It was savage fighting, and many men went down, but those desperate rebels got through by sheer force and weight, and within minutes they were clear of enemies and were running as hard as they could down the rocky hillside.

The legionnaires ran with them, though

they didn't know where they were going or why. All they knew was that they were heading towards the sea, though that didn't seem to offer any particular safety.

Then they found themselves climbing and realised they were ascending the craggy, rocky approach to the promontory which formed the western wall of Dusa harbour. Now it became apparent that in this position the rebels intended to make their last stand.

It was a good site, impregnable from three sides because of the abrupt, smooth-faced rocks. It meant that any attacking force had to come along a narrow neck of land and all the time was exposed to the rebels' fire.

The rebels got down among the rocks and when the Bedouins came flooding in their flowing robes in an impetuous attack upon the promontory, they let them have it. That sent the Bedouins back in headlong retreat, and then nothing happened for an hour or two.

The defenders lay among the sun-scorched rocks, and there wasn't a drop of water among them all. The wounded suffered agonies, and it was heartrending to hear their piteous cries. And many of them died.

Crouched together behind a jutting spur of weather-worn rock the little party of Westerners looked out upon a forlorn scene.

The entire harbour front seemed ablaze now, as a growing wind fanned the flames across the narrow alleys, so that more and more property became engulfed. Mahmoud had started this, but now he was powerless to stop the incendiarism.

A great billowing cloud of black smoke drifted across the town and out onto the desert beyond. With it went showers of burning leaves and grasses and the charred remnants of cloth and paper. The sun came through it all with a blood-red glow, and it seemed at times as though dusk was near because of that restricting haze.

They saw the palace on fire now from end to end, and that was the only thing that brought consolation to those bitter men, the Brotherhood of Tormented Men. They wanted to make a tyrant suffer, and they knew that Mahmoud would be beside himself with fury at the sight of his magnificent palace going up in flames.

They heard one brother whose scarred back told of sufferings under some dictator's lash, say fiercely: 'In all this is justice! Mahmoud set fire to the people's dwellings. So the Greek, our leader, set fire to his in retribution. Allah is wise!' he ended enigmatically.

The legionnaires behind their mouth cloths looked at each other, then, understanding the Greek's act in setting fire to the palace. But they realised that now Mahmoud would have no mercy upon any of them.

Out of the swirling smoke cloud suddenly came a ferocious attack of mounted Bedouins. They had cunningly waited until the wind had drifted smoke very close up to this rocky point, and then had come in with it, taking advantage of it, and suddenly emerging at almost point-blank range and trying to overrun the defences.

Instantly rifles came up and a murderous fusillade blasted out, emptying saddles and felling horses and filling the narrow open space before the rocks with bloody confusion.

So fierce was that volley that the attack wilted immediately, and the survivors turned and fled as frantically as their horses could take them.

As they saw them go, Rube wiped his face and said, with some satisfaction: 'That proves one thing. We're in a good position here. We'll take some diggin' out!'

But the others said nothing. They knew that if Mahmoud had any sense he didn't need to dig them out. He need only sit back and watch and wait — wait for the sun to dig them out for him!

For in this heat they couldn't live more than a few hours without water.

But Mahmoud was determined upon a bloody revenge. He ordered his men into the attack again, though this time they came afoot, in swift little rushes, taking cover behind the fallen horses and even their fallen comrades on that open space before the piled-up rocks of the promontory. This was a more difficult attack to beat off.

The Arabs showed greater initiative

now, so that some put up a fierce covering fire while their companions moved closer. There were losses on both sides then, but Mahmoud's men came steadily forward.

It became obvious that it was only a matter of time before some of those swift-moving desert warriors got in among the rocky defences, and once a breach was made the rest of the Bedouins would come in like a tidal wave.

Rube and his friends watched along the barrels of their Lebels, and fired at the slightest movement, but they saw always that the next movement was a little nearer than before. The Bedouins were skilled in desert warfare, and they knew how to take advantage of the slightest cover. They had learnt their lessons in the last hour, and were profiting by them.

Dimmy fired and saw an Arab twist and roll over and then become still. He said: 'They'll dig us out of these rocks before sundown.'

Joe looked down into the harbour where, no more than half a mile away, sat that rusting steamer. A wisp of vapour told them that steam was still up — but it was no use to them, cooped up here in the blisteringly hot rocks.

Joe sighed, and said: 'If Tex was here . . .'

He didn't finish his sentence, but they knew what he meant. Somehow, they all had tremendous faith in the big legionnaire from Texas, and they had a feeling that no matter how tight the situation, big Tex would have found a way out for them.

But Tex wasn't there.

It was just after Joe had spoken that the Greek came by. He was wriggling in among the rocks, talking to his men and encouraging them and distributing ammunition where it was required. He came up to the little party, which contained the two girls, and they all tried to hide their faces and not be seen.

But the Greek spoke and Rube had to turn to answer him, and Rube's eyes were blue above his attempt to mask his face. The Greek recognised him.

He didn't say anything but went away.

When he had gone Rube said: 'We don't get out of here alive, anyway. That Greek has it in for us. While we're still useful he'll do nothin', but right at the last, before he goes out, we'll go out, too. We're representatives of one of the tyrant powers that this Brotherhood is out to squash!'

His eyes looked grimly at the blazing palace.

He said: 'Remember what the Greek did before we left the palace? That's the sort of thing you expect from the Greek. He's thorough right to the end. If he couldn't have that palace, then Mahmoud wasn't going to have it.'

And Nicky added softly: 'If the Greek can't go on living — ?'

Rube nodded, grim lines on his youthful face. 'He'll see that we don't go on livin', either.'

It wasn't a comforting thought, but they had to lie there and fire when the Bedouins came forward in those quick little rushes, and they grilled under the sun and wondered how soon the end would come.

Hours dragged by, while the town blazed and smoke poured inland over the arid scrub desert. The palace began to collapse, and as a part of the roof caved in and the sparks flew up to the smoky sky, there was something like a cheer from the defenders amongst the rocks. It was a little satisfaction to them to know that they had accomplished something by their revolt, if it was only annoyance to the tyrant Sheik Mahmoud.

The wind momentarily freshened, and drove away the billowing smoke clouds from the harbour area. They saw, in that instant before the smoke closed in again, the massed forces of Mahmoud, and even Mahmoud himself riding in front of his troops and haranguing them.

It was obvious that he had collected all his troops, bringing them from the burning and looting and slaughtering in the town. Clearly he was determined that this time he would finish the ragged rebels on the rocky promontory.

The smoke came rolling back to obscure the picture of those sinister, burnoused Bedouins, massed there in all their awesome might.

Rube said: 'Goldam it, we'll never hold this bunch off this time!' and he looked again down the almost precipitous slope to where the roofs of the sagging warehouses lined the wharf. His eyes lingered on the steamer.

Joe said, sombrely: 'An' there was more of 'em comin' up!' He rubbed a speck of dust off the barrel of his rifle, and crouched lower, and his attitude suggested that he wasn't going out without a desperate fight. 'There was a big bunch all lined up agen the palace wall. Did you see 'em?'

When he had spoken those words they saw Joe begin to lift from his rifle, sitting up and beginning to turn, and there was an incredulous expression on his face as he turned to look at the two crouching girls and his two legionnaire comrades.

He said: 'What am I talkin' about?'

They looked at him, into that flat, battered, good-humoured pan of his, and couldn't understand the expression on his face.

He asked quickly: 'Did you guys see them other fellars? Them Arabs up agen the palace wall?'

He was suddenly so excited that he didn't keep his voice down, and Nicky cautioned him with a quick 'Sssh!'

Rube said: 'What'n heck are you talkin' about?'

Joe's small eyes flickered back towards that smoke pall. He was shaking his head, in the manner of a man who cannot believe what he has seen. He was saying:

'I guess my eyes are playing tricks. You know, jes' for one minute I thought I saw — '

He didn't finish what he 'thought' he saw.

For at that moment Mahmoud mounted his last and most formidable assault.

A thousand wild Bedouin warriors came racing out of the smoke pall. The defenders sighted on the brown, scream- ing faces, upon the hooded horsemen with their flashing scimitars waving above their heads. They poured lead into their ranks, and everywhere Bedouins came off their horses, and some of their mounts went down, and there was a scene of sickening confusion.

But the main force of Bedouins still came on.

The Greek was standing up, recklessly exposing himself in order to encourage the defence. He was shouting to them to keep fighting, to fire on, and he suited the action to his words, lifting his rifle and blazing away at the enemy.

He was shot in the shoulder, and they saw blood stain his *galabier*. It seemed to have no effect on him, and he continued to fire.

The next salvo from the defenders did more damage, and yet it did not stop that charge.

The Bedouins, who had been crawling forward on their hands and knees this last half-hour, came suddenly into the picture. They rose and raced forward, and were so near now that in a second they were at handgrips with the defenders. This caused the fire to slacken upon the charging Bedouin horsemen, and they came on, with renewed savagery in their triumphant cries.

Joe and the other two legionnaires rose and beat off an attack with the butts of their guns. They were lucky, because only a few un-mounted Bedouins came in among the rocks at this point, but farther to their right a strong force had secured a position, and were now going in among the rocks and were attacking the ragged defenders at point-blank range.

The Bedouin horsemen were within twenty or thirty yards of the defences.

Then out of the smoke pall came a rocketing charge of madly-racing horse-men, and a new war cry was added to that of the Bedouins.

They saw in amazement a compact body of well-mounted, well-armed horse-men drive a wedge through that strung-out force of Bedouins along the approach to the promontory. At once there was the bitterest of hand-to-hand fighting, but the impetus of that charge, and the surprise that came with it, drove the Bedouins back and caused them to turn and with-draw towards the palace walls.

Rube shouted in amazement: 'D'you see what I see?'

Joe's excited face came round. 'My eyes didn't play tricks!' he said. 'That's what I thought I saw. Spahis!'

The forces of France had arrived just in time.

The attack was completely discon-certed by the sudden appearance of that ferociously-fighting body of French native cavalry. The ones who had penetrated the rocky defences found themselves cut off now, between two enemies, and those who had been in the rear of the charge were being tumbled over the rocky edge of the point, down onto the buildings below. It was a rout. That much smaller body of men, because of the perfect timing of their charge, had completely defeated a formidable enemy.

It brought renewed hope to some of the defenders at least, and they rose in all their rags and bitterness, and tore into those attackers — those attackers who all in one minute lost their feelings of exultation and triumph.

They were driven back out of the rocks, and then out on to the open space before the promontory, where they turned and fled in abject confusion. The defenders realised that the Spahis were driving Mahmoud's men in complete disorder into the blazing town itself, and then the swirling smoke pall came down and hid the scene, and then the defenders were left alone.

There was no jubilation among the Tormented Men. All their lives they had come to believe that France represented an oppressive tyranny where Arabs were concerned. Because this timely intervention had saved them, they did not change their minds now.

To them it seemed that France had taken advantage of the revolt in the Hejib and was moving in her troops to take over the place. They would, in fact, substitute one tyrant for another, and they hadn't fought and bled just for that end.

The Greek was with his lieutenants, watching into the smoke pall and listening to the sounds of battle. He gave attention to the low, solemn voices of his companions, who thought as he did about the situation. And then he spoke, and his voice was quite gentle.

'We owe this to those accursed legionnaires whom we took prisoner. We should have killed them out of hand.' His eyes were narrowed and searching among the rocks.

'They were part of some plan of France's to bring troops into the Hejib,' he continued. 'They were spies.'

At that an angry murmur rose from those bearded, tattered-robed followers of his, these men who hated tyrants because they had suffered so much beneath them.

And a voice said roughly: 'Let us find them! Let us kill them! They have betrayed us, and they should not be allowed to live and enjoy their triumph!'

The murmur rose to a roar as the word was passed among the remaining defenders, and at once those fierce-looking, bare-footed men turned to find the legionnaires and the infidel girl who travelled with them. They would tear them limb from limb . . .

But when they looked the infidels weren't there.

Suleiman the Hideous was there, but not his friends.

They went up to Suleiman and the Greek said: 'Where did they go?' His eyes were fierce and hostile as he looked at Suleiman, because he knew that Suleiman had forgotten much that he had once known — he had even learned to like the representatives of these accursed Franks.

Suleiman looked at him levelly. He faced up to his leader, and he was not afraid.

He said: 'They went — they slipped away even as that charge by the Spahis began.' And Mahfra had gone with them, he was thinking.

The Greek sneered. 'And why did you not go with your European friends, O Dog Who Cannot Live Without His Masters?'

Suleiman did not lose his temper at that insult, not even with that hostile crowd hemming him in so that he could feel their hot breath fanning his neck and face.

He said, simply: 'They wanted me to go with them. But I would not leave you. My heart is with the Brotherhood, and I am no traitor that I would run away at a time when men of our kind need me.'

He spoke so quietly, so effectively though without any intention of being effective, that his words silenced the critics and shamed the ones who had thought ill of him. For now at once they all remembered that Suleiman the Hideous had been the most faithful and unswerving of the Brotherhood which sought to help the weak and oppressed in the Arab continent.

The anger, unaccustomed to that handsome Greek face, fled swiftly at those words, and the big Arab leader leaned forward and clasped Suleiman by the hand, and there was pressure in that grip which said: 'Forgive me. I should have known you would not leave us.'

And perhaps the Greek knew what it had meant to Suleiman to make that decision to stay there with the Brotherhood. For Suleiman, in moments of confidence, had told his comrade something of his love for Mahfra the peasant maiden, and he had even touched upon the offer of big Tex the legionnaire, to take him to America for plastic surgery.

The Greek greeted Suleiman as a comrade. Yet he was unswerving in his determination to extinguish the legionnaires whom he thought to have been planted among them to act as spies and traitors. There was no doubt in his mind that they were responsible for this invasion by the French.

His blue, un-Arab eyes moved away from Suleiman's big brown ones and went searching on to the smoke-covered cliffside, which gave onto the wharf below. He thought he saw a movement.

He turned to his men and said: 'There are among us men who have served us ill. We have lost Hejib, not to Mahmoud, but to the tyrannous French, and the French agents are still with us.'

His finger was pointing down towards the wharf side.

He said: 'We will finish those spying agents, and then we will take that ship and put out to sea, though God knows where we shall find rest.'

The ragged remnants of the rebel army poured out from the corpse-strewn rocks and went in search of pathways down the steep-sloping hillside. Ahead of them now, running across the bare quayside, they could see the fugitives in their Arab robes. A mighty yell went up from the ragged rebels. It was a shout in which was contained all the frustration of their hopes — it would be poured upon the hapless fugitives running towards the gangplank of that old hulk.

'Kill the infidels!' they shouted, and then recklessly they began to pour down the slope towards the ship.

11

'Go Where Your Heart Desires'

They heard that shout when they were almost up to the rotten old gangplank that bridged the narrow gap between rusting ship and sagging wharf. They were in blazing sunshine now, beyond the range of the swirling smoke.

They had sneaked away down the treacherous paths and gained the warehouse without mishap. And then Rube had gone forward on a scouting expedition, and with bated breath they had watched him run aboard the ship and then disappear. After what seemed an eternity of time he had come back to the gangplank and beckoned to them, and they were just running to meet him when they heard that terrifying shout from above their heads: *'Kill the infidels!'*

They twisted their necks as they ran and looked back and upwards and it seemed to them that those harsh, jagged rocks were alive with leaping forms, as the Arabs came down with reckless haste to get at them.

Rube shouted: 'Come on! The crew want to get away from this port an' they'll man the ship for us.'

He stood aside, his rifle raised to fire at the flood of men who were descending behind the long low warehouses. The others ran aboard the ship. They didn't go below.

The Greek, up on the hillside, saw the danger to his plans — first that the traitors, as he thought them, would escape, and secondly that their own avenue of escape by way of the sea might be deprived them. He wasn't going to see that rusty old ship sailed away right from underneath his nose.

His voice rang out across the intervening distance, and he had a rifle to his shoulder and it was pointing at the blonde American girl who was with the party. He shouted: 'Stand still! One more move and the American girl will die.'

Joe had cast off a rope in the bows.

Dimmy was lifting the big looped rope from off the bollard in the stern. If he let that go the ship would be free from the wharf and might begin to move away of its own accord. But he stood there holding on to the rope because he thought that if he let it go with a betraying splash into the water it might bring a bullet to end Nicky's life. He knew the Greek would carry out his threat, and he couldn't take risks where lovely Nicky's life was concerned.

Others on that hillside had got their rifles up and trained upon the group standing helplessly on the littered deck. Others of the Brotherhood were completing the descent and coming down through the warehouses.

Aboard the ship the legionnaires saw the flood of what seemed hundreds of men pour out and fill the wharf before them. The Greek came down and joined them. The legionnaires' rifles were pointing towards the tattered, unshaven rebels — though there were infinitely more rifles pointing back at them.

The situation was ticklish. One false

move — one too-ready trigger-finger — and bullets would blaze from either party and there would be death right there on the quayside.

The legionnaires had no illusions, however. They knew that they didn't stand a chance. Yet they kept their rifles directed towards that menacing crowd, because if they were going out then they would take some of these blood-lusting Arabs with them.

The Greek came forward, and he showed his great courage by doing so. For at once the legionnaires pointed their rifles at him and he knew that he would die first, even before the legionnaires, if trouble broke out.

He said: 'We are coming aboard. Resistance is useless. If you attempt to hold us back you will die — and your womenfolk with you.'

Rube said, harshly: 'We know we're gonna die, anyway. You don't need to try kiddin' us on that point, brother!'

The Greek said: 'You are going to die, O son of a foreign race.' Then his eyes flickered towards the two girls, who were crouching together against a hatch. 'But we need not be so brutal to these two women. If you put down your guns we will see that no harm comes to them.'

It was curious that the Greek was an enemy who would take their lives, and yet they knew they could trust his word. Rube looked at Joe, and licked his lips. Then Nicky called out desperately: 'You can't do it, Rube. You can't just give yourselves to these men without a fight. They will kill you as soon as they come aboard.'

For there was no mistaking the menacing intentions of that mob that thronged only five yards away across the gangplank.

Rube listened to her, and then very slowly he grounded the butt of his gun. He said, levelly: 'I'm takin' you at your word, brother. You have promised not to harm these gals. Okay, I give myself up to you.' Joe dropped his rifle with a clatter to the deck. He said: 'Okay, I'm with you, Rube. I won't fight if these gals can be spared.'

Dimmy let go of the rope and it fell

into the water, and he covered the action by putting his rifle down at his feet. The ship stayed where it was. The gangplank, for the moment anyway, was holding it in position.

The Greek put one foot onto the narrow gangplank. There was a surging movement of the crowd behind him, as they all prepared to step aboard the ship — some to follow the Greek across the gangplank and others simply to jump the gap. The legionnaires aboard the ship knew they were within minutes, perhaps seconds, of death. They saw no mercy in the faces across from them.

Mahfra and Nicky were standing together, crying in agony because they didn't want to see what they would see.

Then a man rode with a mighty clatter of hooves on to the stone-flagged end of the wharf. He came riding hell-for-leather, though his horse was doubly burdened, and as he rode he shouted and his voice was not an Arab's.

It halted them, there on the quayside. They turned and looked and saw . . . the legionnaire from Texas, his neck curtain fluttering as he rode, the blue of his tunic almost obliterated under the dust of the desert.

He came riding boldly right up to that crowd, so that it parted as he forced his horse towards the gangplank where the Greek stood raised above the heads of his fellows.

Fascinated, the legionnaires aboard the ship saw that another wearing the blue uniform of the Legion was lying across the horse in front of Tex. There was a sob of joy from Nicky as she saw this big man whom she loved, and whom she thought had died and was lost to her. And a smile came to Joe's face that was bigger than any that had ever been there before — and he was normally a man of big smiles.

Rube merely exclaimed: 'Tex, by heck!' And Dimmy watched with beaming face, but without saying anything. Tex was surrounded by fierce-eyed, hungry-jawed men who jostled right up to his stirrups. And yet he sat there as if he had no thought of enemies within miles of him. Instead, he leaned forward in his saddle and he spoke with dramatic urgency to the Greek, and his words were so unexpected that it silenced the growlmg murmurs that had begun to rise from the mob at his appearance.

Tex shouted: 'What in the blazes are you doin' down here, Greek? Don't you realise this is your big opportunity?'

Tex swung down, right there among the fierce-eyed rebels. He dragged the bound body of the uniformed man off his horse and slung it over his shoulder as if he were a child. They saw that the face was Sturmer's. Tex strode up to the Greek and went on talking vigorously.

'Mahmoud's men are in flight. Mahmoud himself is dead — I killed him. This is your chance to consolidate your position here in the Hejib.' He gestured towards the smoking ruins of the town. 'The people don't want Mahmoud or his kind any more, and I reckon you and your people will form a better sort of government than anything Mahmoud could provide. Mebbe,' said the big Texan, his grey eyes sweeping over the motley throng, 'this will be one Arab State where there is justice an' mercy, an' a chance of a better life for the poorer people.'

The Greek wasn't speaking. Neither was he believing what he was hearing.

Rube shouted: 'Tex, watch out! The Greek thinks we played traitor on the rebels and brought the French in to take over the State.'

Tex just said abruptly: 'Don't be a damned fool, Greek! Get your men out right away into the town and beat up every last remainin' Mahmoud supporter!'

'The French — ' the Greek said abruptly, but there was a dawning hope along with the suspicion in his blue eyes.

'The French?' The big legionnaire with the bound and helpless Nazi officer over his shoulder gestured impatiently. 'There's no French army here in the Hejib. I brought in a couple of hundred Spahis, and they've routed Mahmoud, but right now I reckon they're high-tailin' it out of the territory. They're not in force to try anythin' like grabbin' the Hejib for France.'

The Greek moved a little pace forward — quickly, involuntarily, eagerly . . .

'If I could believe you, O Americano — '
he almost whispered.

That handsome head lifted to look over
the smoke-enveloped town. In his eyes
was desire. Here at the last moment there
might be success to the Brotherhood's
plans — here they might create a true
democracy, and build from the ruins of
this squalid Arab town. They might
provide a better place for the people to
live in, and that was what had started this
adventure.

And yet he couldn't, didn't dare
believe.

His eyes swung down and met the big
Texan's. He said, and his voice was as
harsh as it could ever be: 'I do not trust
you, you men who wear this uniform of
an oppressor state!'

Big Tex looked grimly at him and
said: 'I wear this uniform not because I
wanted to war against the Arabs. I joined
the Legion because I wanted to bring
this man to justice before an international court.

'This man is wanted for crimes against
humanity. France would not give him up,

because it is a tradition of France not to surrender men who have joined their Foreign Legion. I have risked my life, and my comrades have risked theirs, too, in an effort to capture this General Sturmer and take him out of the country.'

He looked at the old steamer.

'I could get him away and take my friends with me if you stood aside and let us use this ship, which is no longer of use to you.'

The Greek said: 'I still cannot trust you.'

Tex lost his temper and shouted impatiently: 'You have a chance to clean up this town and get yourselves in control before any of Mahmoud's lieutenants begin to try to take over. And you go on talkin' here as if our few lives are of importance, anyway!'

He was so palpably sincere in what he was saying that there were men among that crowd — those few who understood this foreign language — who murmured and were plainly persuaded by what he said.

But the Greek was a man slow to lose

the suspicion of years. He stood on the gangplank, and while he was there he was a barrier to their hopes. Behind him the three legionnaires and their two girl companions listened and in their hearts was anguish because it seemed impossible that this Arab leader of the brethren would ever yield and show them compassion.

Then a big man came pushing to the edge of the wharf, and he was a man who by his face showed that he had suffered more than anyone there at the hands of tyrants.

It was Suleiman the Hideous.

Suleiman, with his big bare feet and his long tattered *galabier* and knitted skull-cap, was as unlovely a figure as anyone could look upon. And yet there was a quietness, a calmness and a dignity about the man that created its own respect. They listened to him as he spoke.

He said: 'There was once a time when I would have killed these American Legionnaires even though they had saved my life. I, too, did not believe there could be any good in these men of an alien race.

'But in these last weeks I have changed my mind, and now I am their friend and I believe in them and I trust them. I believe that all they say is true and we should act upon the advice of this American. I say that we should forget petty vengeance, and in gratitude for the help these people have given us we should let them go with their prisoner as they desire.'

Suleiman's hand waved towards the town.

'Let us go out now and gather the people together under the flag of the diagonal cross! Let us go forward where we left off, routing our enemies before they can gather to defeat us again, and let us this day begin to build a new and better state here in the Hejib.

'I will stay with you, O Greek, and in staying my life will be forfeit if you find that after all these foreigners have tricked you with their tongues. You can kill me if you find that in fact the French have been brought here with the intention of holding the Hejib as part of their empire.'

Saying which the big ugly Arab became

silent, standing there with his empty hands down at his side. His comrades looked at him, and then slowly the Greek came off the gangplank and stepped ashore. He stood on one side, his eyes holding Tex's, as the big American legionnaire moved to pass him, bearing that bound figure on his broad shoulder.

As they passed neither spoke, but their eyes looked into each other's, and there was perhaps a salute in them, as of one brave man to another.

Tex walked across the gangplank. He had just reached the deck when the gangway slipped away from the ship's side as the vessel swung with the tide and came a few yards away from the wharf. Arab sailors peeped above the hatchway, and then went below when they saw they were free of the shore. In a moment the engines would begin to revolve and the old hooker would move out to sea and away from this town where so much blood-shed had occurred.

But four legionnaires and two girls looked back at that throng upon the quayside — at the Greek with his rough-looking

251

followers . . . and at the big lonely figure of Suleiman, who had been such a friend and companion to them over these desert trails of the past weeks.

Mahfra was crying, and she was whispering: 'O Suleiman!' It seemed that for all his appearance Suleiman had found favour with this peasant girl whom he had helped in so many ways.

Nicky was in big Tex's arms and they were looking towards the shore, and Nicky was whispering, brokenly: 'Oh, Tex, why has Suleiman to stay behind?'

The gap was widening. The wharf was receding.

And then Suleiman ran and took a mighty leap and was on the deck with them and grasping them by the hands, and it seemed that that big man who had suffered so much without a murmur was near to tears — tears of happiness.

And no one on that wharfside fired at him or tried to do him any harm.

Suleiman was saying: 'The Greek said to me: 'I find it is in my heart to trust these foreigners. Go, O Suleiman, go where your heart desires'!'

The Greek had found generosity in his soul in the end.

The engines leapt to life at that, and a foam appeared at their stern, and the ship began to glide away with an Arab seaman suddenly appearing at the helm. It was a signal to the Brotherhood to depart and go into the town of smoke and flame to start the work of building a new and better place for the oppressed Arab people.

They watched from the deck until Dusa was a speck upon the horizon. Then they turned, with darkness falling softly upon them, and Tex said: 'It's the start of a new life for a lot of us.' He was thinking of his ranch in Texas — thinking of Nicky, who would come and live with him and love that life on the cattle range.

And Suleiman . . .

Suleiman was standing near to Mahfra and yet not daring to go too close with that twisted, ugly face of his.

But soon that would be all right. Soon clever surgeons would remove the ravages that pain had brought to that face; they would restore to him the appearance he had once borne. Then Mahfra would want him, and that was how it should be.

Only ex-Nazi General Sturmer, lying bound on the deck, viewed with pessimism a future that was bright for these others.

THE END

Other titles in the
Linford Mystery Library:

ONE MURDER AT A TIME

Richard A. Lupoff

They'd been an odd couple, brought together by a murder investigation and discovering that they had an amazing chemistry . . . Hobart Lindsey is a suburban, middle-class, conservative-minded claims adjuster and Marvia Plum is a tough city cop who has fought her way up from the street. But now the couple have split and gone their own ways, both pursuing a series of mysterious crimes. Then fate throws them together again, reuniting them at the scene of a lurid murder . . .

THE 'Q' SQUAD

Gerald Verner

An habitual criminal attempts to snatch
Penelope Hayes' handbag, yet is appre-
hended and charged. Two months later,
she's abducted and chloroformed — and
again rescued by the police. This time
her assailant escapes with her handbag. It seems that the wave of daring
criminal gang robberies across London
is somehow connected to Penelope's
handbag — despite her denials that it
contained anything of value. Then she
disappears again — and the police have
a murder investigation on their hands . . .

MR. BUDD INVESTIGATES

Gerald Verner

Provost Captain Slade Moran arrives from Fort Benson, Colorado, to investigate the disappearance of an army payroll and its military secret. A grim trail has taken him to the empty payroll coach and its murdered escort, with one soldier mysteriously missing. Moran is led to Moundville where he's confronted by desperate men plotting to steal a gold mine. Embroiled in double-cross and mayhem, Moran fears he will fail in his duty. Against all odds, can he succeed?